UNION OF SIN

EDEN SUMMERS

DEDICATION

To those naughty readers who came back for more after their first shot of sin. This one's for you.

CHAPTER ONE

T.J. sat in his car, transfixed with a sight so familiar it brought a piercing ache to his sternum—his wife. Cassie's blonde hair gleamed from the early morning kiss of the sun. Her full-length dress clung to her every curve. With one glimpse, she made everything else cease to exist. It was only him and her. The two of them. No road too long or river too wide to stop him from claiming her.

At least that's how it had been...before he'd left. Now the few yards separating them, from his car to her position at the neighborhood park swing set, was as vast as the Atlantic.

This morning was his final farewell. His silent thank you to the heavens for giving him the few years of paradise he'd shared with this beautiful woman. Their time together was nothing short of a fairy tale—love at first sight, wedded bliss and the promise of a perfect future.

But they'd never received their happily ever after. He'd fucked up. Not once, many times. He just hadn't realized the extent until it was too late. Until he was separated from her, away from the mesmerizing spell of her love.

1

He'd almost destroyed this woman. He still could if he hung around.

Neither of them had seen it coming. They'd been consumed by happiness. The drug of euphoria had blinded them from reality.

Not anymore.

T.J. watched as Cassie guided her niece from the swing set and they began to walk from the playground hand in hand. Essentially, he was stalking her. He knew she took the little girl to the park every other Saturday morning. He also knew as soon as she returned the child to her mother, she would walk the two blocks to T.J.'s home.

Their home.

He followed her, inching the car forward with each of her steps. He made sure to lurk behind the street corners until she was out of sight before he'd move farther. When Cassie reached the road to their house, his stomach hollowed. A car was waiting in their driveway. A car he'd arranged to be there.

Her footsteps faltered as she approached, and when a man dressed in a tailored black suit slid from the car, she stopped abruptly. There was an exchange of words, but he was too far away to read lips. He didn't need to though. The envelope in the guy's hand said it all. The resulting anguish on his wife's stunning face cemented what had just happened.

The divorce papers were now firmly in her grasp. He couldn't help inching forward, taking her suffering head-on. He deserved her pain. Her spite. He wanted to feel it. To suffer as much as possible.

She wouldn't realize this was necessary. She probably never would. And that was okay. He could live with the responsibility. He already had for months.

The black Mercedes reversed from his driveway, pulled onto the road and disappeared into the distance. All he could do was stare. And suck in the pain he could see ebbing from his wife in tidal waves. She was shaking, clasping the envelope tightly, her gaze fixed on the green grass at her feet.

He inched the car forward, consoling himself with her proximity. She was so close. He could almost feel the delicate strands of her hair through his fingers. Could almost smell the perfume he'd bought her for their last wedding anniversary.

He'd kill to touch her again. To soothe the sorrow from her eyes with his kiss. With his passion.

But that would never happen. Not once. Not ever.

He focused over her shoulder, needing a distraction, and settled his gaze on the home they'd built with their bare hands. From the foundation to the curtains, the landscaping to the damn mailbox. All of it had been created with hard work, determination and love. Lots of love.

Cheesy, yes, but it had been one of those moments in life where he'd thought he'd actually achieved greatness. He'd had a wife he adored, a brand-new home to shelter the family they planned to create, and their German shepherd, Bear, to complete the package.

It seemed like yesterday they were arguing about the color to paint the internal walls. He'd remained adamant about his choice up until the moment they'd begun the arduous chore. Then, like always, the gorgeous smile Cassie had greeted him with as he'd opened the paint can had made her crappy selection worthwhile.

That smile undid him. Or it had. It felt like years had passed since she'd dazzled him with her happiness. A day without her resembled an eternity. So, the pain of the months spent separated couldn't be described.

He missed sweeping her off her feet—physically and emotionally. He missed the way she squealed when he tickled her ankles. Most of all, he missed feeling the softness of her curves against his body as he fell asleep.

He'd never get back to that place.

What they had was gone. Dead and buried. He'd killed all hope for a future. He'd wasted her time and ruined her life. He couldn't do it anymore. It had to stop.

He slammed his palms against the steering wheel and squeezed his eyes shut to fight the burn. Soon it would be over. Their court appearance was in less than a month. The documents in her hand explained all the assets he was giving her—the car, the house, their dog. She would continue to be financially stable if she retained her job. She would be safe and secure. And maybe, one day, happy.

The next twenty-seven days were going to kill him, though. Every other day afterward, too. But they could both start over after the heartache eased. Cassie could focus on working up the ranks in her hotel administration position. Maybe she'd find a new man. Someone else to love her. To hold her. To see those achingly brilliant smiles and wipe away her tears.

"*Shit*." He needed to get out of here before he crumpled completely.

He opened his eyes, blinked to clear his vision and stared at the flawless woman as she squinted directly at his car. *Oh, fuck.*

The envelope dropped to the ground as her hands fell to her sides. She stood there, lower lip trembling, chest convulsing, as her misery hit him tenfold.

"*Divorce papers?*" Her voice cracked as she yelled.

Jesus. He'd pushed her too far. Cassie was quiet, composed and polite, at least for every other day of their marriage. Right now, she was causing a scene, alerting their nosy neighbors to her imminent breakdown.

He shouldn't have come. He should've gone to Shot of Sin, drowned in a bottle of something expensive and relied on

Leo and Brute to get him home. Instead, he was cutting the ignition and sliding from the car, unable to stand her misery.

He strode for her, determined to explain that life would be better this way. It had to be better. *She* had to be better. He couldn't exist if she wasn't.

"You're a coward, Tate Jackson." She didn't move, didn't budge as her lips trembled. "A weak, pathetic coward who can't even spare his wife the dignity of telling her he wants a divorce. You had to get some stranger to inform me."

He increased his pace up the drive. "Lower your voice."

Her eyes widened, her mouth parted slightly. Then she slowly raised her chin. "*No.*" Her voice was a breath. "That tone has no effect on me anymore. Those papers make it so." She waved a hand in the direction of the envelope on the grass. "How could you?"

He stopped in front of her, rested his hand against her upper arm and tried to lead her inside, away from prying eyes.

"Don't you dare." She slid away from him, her gentle features contorting into a glare. She'd never looked at him like this before. It was foreign. Hard to take.

He would give his soul to drag her forward into his chest and comfort her in his arms until the harsh reality faded. He missed her. God, how he missed her. Her scent lingered in the air, tempting his restraint. And those lips... He released a huff of frustration. The way she kissed would never be comparable. Her loving heart would forever be a part of him.

Cassie sucked in a breath, straightened her shoulders and met his gaze head-on. "Don't do this to us, T.J." Her light blue eyes pleaded more than her words ever could. "*Please.* I still love you. I'll *always* love you."

He was thankful for the rapid scampering of nails against cement, then the loud bark of Bear as he voiced his greeting from the side gate. They remained silent through the echoing noise, his focus unable to leave her face. Time stopped, and the understanding of why he was doing this became blurry.

She was still the most mesmerizing woman he'd ever seen. The dress she wore clung to all her delicious curves, outlining breasts and hips that had tormented his dreams. The nipples beading against the thin cotton made his mouth dry, and he wished like hell he hadn't noticed. But it was her eyes, the sky-blue depths welling with unshed tears that tore him apart.

"T.J." Her voice barely registered over the throbbing in his ears. Her hand came up between them, her palm creeping toward his chest.

He stepped back, sensing the burn her contact would ignite. Her delicate touch would undo him. It would send him spiraling with a one-way ticket to the courthouse to cancel the divorce proceedings.

She was his heart. The one woman who brought out his darkest desires and forged a sexual appetite he couldn't ignore. She allowed him the freedom to become the man he always wanted to be, yet at the same time made him wish he was someone else entirely. Someone better. Someone worthy of a woman so forgiving and sweet.

She dropped her hand slowly to her side and Bear quietened.

Her gaze lowered, her light lashes fluttering down toward her blushed cheeks. "I can't live without you, Tate."

Fucking hell. She was gutting him, slicing open his chest and letting his insides fall to the ground. How could he walk away? How could he leave her, knowing this time he'd never return?

"It's for the best," he lied.

For Cassie, it would be the truth, but from this moment on, he'd forever be less of a man for losing this woman from his life.

~

*C*assie held her breath, agonizing over the resolution in her husband's tight features. He was adamant. Confident in his decision. For the life of her, she couldn't understand why.

She pressed her lips together, vowing not to shed another tear, at least not in front of him. *Goddamnit.* She wanted to shake him. To slap him out of whatever spell he was under and make him remember the happiness they'd once shared. She'd been content. Their honeymoon phase had never faded. It had only morphed into a deeper connection where T.J. had showed her a whole new side of herself.

He awakened her to life. To love. To pleasure. And although it had hurt when he'd packed his bags and told her he needed time apart, she'd known, without doubt, that their commitment to one another couldn't be extinguished by a few months' separation.

Love like theirs was a gift. One she couldn't go without.

"The divorce can't be legal. I won't agree to it."

"I don't need your consent, Cass, the court date has already been set."

"That's impossible." The blood drained from her face, making her dizzy. She shook her head, in disbelief or defiance, she wasn't sure. There was no way their separation fulfilled the legal requirements for what he was doing. "You moved out six months ago. I'm sure we need to be apart for twelve before you can file for divorce."

His gaze softened, his brown eyes filling with pity. "I stopped sleeping in your bed a year ago. That's enough for the courts."

Her heart stopped, and pain ricocheted through her ribs, growing with intensity. She pressed a hand to her chest, trying to alleviate the agony that wouldn't lessen. It

7

continued to evolve, moving to her limbs, weakening her knees.

"Why?" The word skittered from her trembling lips.

The answer was clear without him having to voice it. His warped sense of masculine protection had taken its toll, leaving him a slave to the guilt he had no right to feel.

"Is this still about that stupid club?" The one fateful night where their excitement to experiment had gone too far.

"This is about me." His tone was low. Unwavering. "Nobody else."

"Liar." She knew the truth. They'd had one bad experience. One testing, heartbreaking experience, and now he was ready to quit. "You still haven't let go of what happened."

"You're right." He inclined his head. "I can't. I never will. But the divorce is about much more than that."

In her mind, she was screaming, clawing at the beautiful eyes she'd gazed into on her wedding day, the same ones she'd imagined would peer down at their first child with intense adoration if they were ever blessed with a baby.

"I'm sorry." He pressed his lips tight.

Sorry? He hadn't even given her the opportunity to repair what was broken. He hadn't even tried.

"Sorry doesn't cut it." She shook her head again, vehement this time.

Twelve months ago, he'd started sleeping on the sofa, breaking her heart with his need for space—for clarity she couldn't give. Six months later, he'd strode from their house needing more distance.

At the time, she'd thought it was best to adhere to his wishes. His love for her was still evident in his eyes, his words, his touch. So, she'd let him go, giving him what he needed. Months and months of space where she cried herself to sleep for nights on end, not once pushing him to return.

Now she wasn't so stupid. She wouldn't succumb to his requests again.

The pain in her chest morphed into anger, red-hot and all consuming. Every inch of her was filled with determination, every nerve thrumming with the need to win this battle.

"I'll fight it. I'll tell the judge we haven't been separated that long." Her voice rose. "I'll do whatever necessary."

His jaw ticked. "We both know you won't lie under oath."

Maybe not. He knew her too well.

"We never went to counseling. I'll tell the court I want to try that first." There had to be another way. A different option.

"You didn't go, Cass, but I did." He hung his head, hammering another nail into the coffin of their marriage.

"You went to counseling without me?" Her words barely registered. This didn't make sense. They were perfect together. They'd shared everything from explicit sexual fantasies to their greatest fears and everything in between. His actions didn't compute. They'd only made one wrong decision. One mistake, and now she was meant to give up on their future. There had to be more.

"Is there another woman?" Nausea edged up her throat. "Is that what this is about? You've found someone else?"

She died a thousand deaths waiting for his reply. Her mind went on a psychotic bender, picturing him cheating with beautiful women. Skinny, flawless women. Ones with slight curves and perky breasts.

She sucked in a breath. "That's it, isn't it? You've been unfaithful."

"No." The word was emphatic as he glanced at her through the loose strands of dark-brown hair falling around his chocolate eyes.

Her body sagged, and she clasped her hands to stop them

from shaking. She believed him. She had no clue why, but she clung to the sincerity in his gaze. She had to.

"Then why, T.J.? You can't leave me because of one mistake."

"Cassie." Her name was a plea.

"Don't *Cassie* me. You need to explain how you can walk away so easily. It doesn't make sense." She no longer cared for the heartache etched in his features. All her sympathy had washed away under her own pain. She needed answers. Now.

His features crumpled as he turned his focus back to his car parked yards down the road. "This is about me wanting the best for you." He ran a rough hand through his hair and clutched the back of his head. "You deserve better."

"*Bullshit.* This is about one night, and one night only. Can't you see how ridiculous that is?"

"Lower your voice."

His commanding growl sent a myriad of heated memories to the forefront. She loved that dominant voice. But she'd never obey him again. Not unless they remained husband and wife.

"I didn't mean for this to happen." He stepped back, placing agonizing distance between them. "Hurting you is the last thing I want to do."

"Then stop."

"I have. That's what the divorce is all about. After you pick yourself up, you'll realize this is the best path for your future."

"The best path?" She glared. "No. The best path for me will always lead to my husband."

He raised his chin, met her gaze. "Trust me on this."

She stared at him, noticing the added lines of strain around his eyes, the downward turn of heavenly lips she was too used to seeing curved in the opposite direction.

"There is no more trust." She tried not to let his

retreating steps make her want to buckle under the weight of loss.

T.J. acknowledged her bitter words with a nod and turned on his heels. He thought he was walking out of her life. Out of her heart. Yet, he could never leave. Even when he'd stopped sleeping in their bed, she'd still felt him beside her. And when he'd left their home, she'd clung to the thought of him, waiting for his return.

She would never lose faith in their marriage, no matter what lay ahead. The only problem was, after twelve months of despair, she didn't know how much fight she had left in her to battle for what they both deserved.

CHAPTER TWO

"*N*ice to see you, stranger."

T.J. swung around to face the playful voice he barely recognized over the heavy dance music. "Hey, sassy. Long time no see."

"Sassy?" Shay raised a brow and quirked her lips. "First time you've called me that."

"If the shoe fits." He nudged her arm and continued walking toward the guarded doorway leading to the private area downstairs. A Shot of Sin, the dance club he owned with his two best friends, Leo and Brute, was too noisy for him tonight. He was still adrift after seeing Cassie this morning. He needed grounding, and he wasn't going to get it from working behind a bustling bar. The only other option, now that their Taste of Sin restaurant was closed for the evening, was Vault of Sin.

Shay shrugged. "True." Her smile was genuine, full of mischief he'd grown to enjoy. "So, what's with the request to work downstairs? Leo told me that part of the business wasn't your forte."

And so the inquisition began.

He came to a stop in front of the security guard situated at the entry to the staircase leading downstairs and gave a nod of appreciation as the man opened the door. The Vault, hidden below the main floor of Shot of Sin, was a private club where members had no intention of dancing and every motivation to get naked and participate in more carnal exercise.

The sex club had never been his favorite place to work because of his commitment to Cassie. She knew what happened behind the closed doors, and although he'd sensed her discomfort, she'd never stipulated he couldn't fulfill this part of his ownership duties.

He'd taken it upon himself to distance his time from the sexually explicit Vault of Sin. He did it as a mark of respect to the woman he adored, especially since they'd never had the opportunity to enjoy the area together. Their problems had started before the sex-club part of his business had been established. And once the doors had opened, he hadn't been able to bring himself to invite her in.

Now his presence didn't seem to matter so much.

"It's quieter down here," he murmured.

Shay followed him into the dimly lit staircase and the guard closed the door behind them. Together they descended, passing pictures of couples on the walls, naked bodies entwined in different sexual positions that only endeavored to remind him of his wife.

"It's quieter at the moment because nobody is down here. But it won't be for long." Shay chuckled. "Some of the clientele are noisy fuckers, and I mean that literally."

He withheld a groan. "I knew what you meant."

Her smile grew as they reached the basement floor. "Do you want to get the lights while I set up the adult entertainment? The first guests will arrive soon."

"Sure." He entered the pin code securing the door at the

end of the hall and held the heavy wood open for her to proceed him into Vault of Sin. While Shay played with the television set in the newbie lounge, he dragged his feet to the main room and flicked the switches on the wall beside the bar. Florescent lights off, mood lighting on.

Truth be told, Cassie would've loved it down here. He supposed that was one of their problems in the first place. He'd shaped her to like what he liked. To adore the depravity he adored. She hadn't been that type of woman when they'd met. She was innocent. Almost pure. He'd shown her the far reaches of sexual desire, not once realizing he was molding her into someone else until it was too late.

A click sounded in the next room, followed by hearty moans and guttural groans from the large television screen Shay was setting up. The noise was far more prevalent than it would be once guests arrived and created the sexual sounds for themselves. The mental image should've awakened his arousal. Instead, he felt dirty. Depraved. A cheat.

He doubted the latter would ever fade.

When he did finally move on, it wouldn't be pretty. He'd always be emotionally committed to Cassie, and he knew his self-respect would be at an all-time low if he shared himself with another.

In his pitiful delusions, he'd even pondered the idea of paying a high-class escort to be the first. Emotions wouldn't be involved that way. It would be a job—for him to get over his wife and for his escort to pay the bills. Win-win. He even had a business card in his wallet. A constant reminder that moving on was a phone call away. Only he couldn't bring himself to dial the number.

"You okay, big guy?" Shay came up behind him.

"All good," he lied. He was dying inside, sinking into purgatory.

He seated himself at the bar, refrained from reaching for a

bottle of Grey Goose and zoned out while Shay polished glasses and checked the beer taps to see if they were in working order. Time moved without him, the world not caring he was falling apart with each second that ticked by.

Patrons arrived in perfectly choreographed intervals. As the night dragged on, people came, literally, and went. He didn't know who or when. He scoped the rooms once or twice, shuffling his feet as he made sure all participation was above board and consensual. But nobody infiltrated his consciousness. Nothing invaded his thoughts. Nothing except Cassie.

"I love you," someone said behind him.

He winced, pushing through the heartache as he remembered the first time his wife uttered those words. He'd fallen for her long before that. Weeks, maybe even months prior to her declaration. He'd kept his adoration to himself, not willing to project his feelings onto her when he wasn't entirely sure she felt the same way.

She had though.

In the sweetest possible way, she'd whispered those words to him. "I love you, Tate. We were made for each other."

"And always will be," he mouthed the words he'd spoken, seeing her image in his mind.

She'd smiled, her cheeks lifting, tiny dimples showing. The sun rose and set in those features. If only he could go back. Change the path. Tweak their outcome.

"Make love to me. Show me you love me, too."

Her words had filled him with determination. He'd do anything for her, including making the world around them vanish as he devoted his mind, body and soul to her. "I don't know how I lived without you."

Sappy dialogue had never been his calling card. Yes, he prided himself on being a gentleman, but it wasn't until Cassie that he'd truly understood the power words yielded.

Over time, the memory of his touch would fade. He could only hope she'd never lose the recollection of the softly uttered endearments he gifted to her.

"You didn't," she'd murmured. "You existed. Life didn't start until there was you and me."

T.J. brushed his lips over hers, sliding his hands under her shirt. The softness of her body undid him. He liked curves, and Cassie had them in abundance. He lifted her, cradling her in his arms as he strode to their bedroom.

He placed her on her feet and undid the buttons of his shirt. "There's a present for you in my top drawer."

Her gaze narrowed, her angelic eyes reading him as her lips curved in awareness. He'd done this before—placed items in his bedside table for her. Always of a sexual nature. Vibrators, dildos, nipple stimulators, anything and everything to improve her enjoyment.

She turned, slid out his top drawer and frowned. "What is it?"

"Take it out and have a look." Her innocence did funny things to him. He always got a kick out of introducing her to new pleasures, testing her boundaries, awakening her to something different. It was the reason their sexuality had gone too far, too fast. He couldn't help himself.

"What am I meant to do with it?" She picked up the C-shaped toy between her thumb and forefinger and examined it with a frown.

"The smaller end goes inside you, against your G-spot. The thicker part curls around your pubic bone to rest on your clit."

She shot him a look, her lips curved in a smirk. "Sounds like a lot of fun for me. Where do you come into all this?"

"I'll come. Don't worry about that." He stepped forward, lifting the flimsy material of her shirt over her head, revealing her sensuous breasts contained in a white lace bra. She lowered her skirt to the ground, gifting him with the exposure of matching panties while her heated gaze ate him up.

"Take off your underwear."

She inclined her head, lowering her focus in submission. Elegant fingers gripped her waistband, baring more tempting flesh—the trimmed strip of hair at her mound, the glimpse of pussy lips, her thighs, her generous ass.

"The bra, too."

She raised her brows. "I'm getting there." Her hands wove around her back, working the clasp before the material fell free and drifted to the floor. "Is that better?"

"You should never wear clothes," he uttered the truth. Cassie was made for a nudist colony. For the admiring glances from men and women alike.

She hugged her stomach, succumbing to doubt.

"Don't ever cover yourself." With a gentle finger, he tapped her wrists in a silent command. "I want this inside you." He motioned to the toy in her hand and gripped the narrow, thinner end. Slowly, he guided the rounded tip down her body, over her abdomen, straight to the apex of her thighs. "I want to watch you take it from here."

The tops of her cheeks darkened to the most precious shade of pink. "How do I turn it on?"

"You don't, my love." He was confident calling her that now. And always would be. She was his love. His one and only. "Just put it inside that gorgeous pussy of yours and I'll do the rest."

She nodded, the slight, almost nervous movement making the protective part of him explode in the need to bring confidence to her actions. She was style. She was grace. She was everything and anything a man like him could wish for. Her inability to see her value or strut around showing it off astounded him.

With her hand still clutching the toy, she crawled onto the bed and rested on her back. He couldn't tear his gaze away—didn't want to, never would—as she closed her eyes briefly and slipped the black object into her pussy.

"Perfect." The word was a whisper through his drying mouth.

"I *do* try my best."

There it was, the brief spark, the tiny glimmer of sexual confidence that drove him to madness. She was at home in his bed.

He pulled his phone from the back pocket of his pants and scrolled to the most recently downloaded app. The software that had come with the product allowed him to control the device remotely. From her side, to another state, or even another country, he could initiate her pleasure with the touch of a button. All he had to do was decide whether he wanted to stimulate her G-spot, her clit, or both at once, and at what ferocity.

"Let's take our time, shall we." He wasn't one to rush. He enjoyed building her arousal, stoking her into a craze before allowing her to succumb to bliss. With a quick double-tap, the external stimulator hummed to life, wrenching a gasp from her throat.

"Jesus." Her eyes widened.

He chuckled as he shucked his pants, leaving them in a heap at his feet. "You like?"

"As always." The shock left her features, replaced with a sultry, dreamy gleam in her eye. "I still don't get how you're going to benefit from this."

"Your pleasure is my pleasure." He'd play the selfless card a little longer, until he couldn't take it anymore. Then he'd inform her the toy and his cock could both easily be accommodated inside her body. He'd make sure of it.

He tapped his phone screen again, twice more on the

external stimulation and once for the vibrations to start against her G-spot.

"Oh, holy hell, T.J." She grasped at the quilt, arching her back, closing her eyes.

One day, he wanted to lay all his gifts out on the bed—the cuffs, the massage oils, the fetish restrains, the anal plug and vibrators. One by one, he'd use them all, sating her to the point of exhaustion before finally taking his own pleasure inside her breathtaking body.

"T.J.?" Cassie began to writhe, her tone foreign. Distorted with lust.

"Hmm?" He smiled down at her, sensing her apprehension, feeling it spur to life underneath his ribcage, because just like her pleasure, her worry was his to own as well.

"T.J.?"

Her voice became distant, her image darkening. Fading. He squinted, blinked and tried to focus back on the heaven before him as it continued to drift away.

"*T.J.*"

Shit. He snapped out of the memory and frowned up at Shay. She stood beside the light switch, her hair more frazzled than it was moments ago, her brown eyes tired. "Can you help me pack up?"

He shot a glance over his shoulder to the now empty room. Seconds ago, naked bodies had writhed in wanton abandon behind him. The sex swing had been in use, the space filled with chatter and sexual delirium.

He was losing his goddamn mind.

"Yeah." He cleared his throat and slid from the stool, thankful for the bar that currently hid the dying bulge in his pants. "What needs to be done?"

Shay looked at him, *really* looked at him. Her brow was

furrowed, her mouth set in a tight line. "Where the hell have you been the last three hours?"

He broke eye contact, the uncomfortable shiver of exposure drifting down his spine. "I guess I got caught up in my thoughts."

"About your wife?" She grabbed a yellow cloth from the counter and began polishing the bar.

"About life in general. I've got a lot on my mind."

He strode for the first private area and flicked on the fluorescent light, not in the mood to talk. The large bed in the middle of the room was mussed, the cushions scattered in varying positions on the mattress and floor. One by one, he picked them up, removing their cloth covers and throwing the material toward the doorway. He didn't usually partake in cleaning. The contracted business they paid handsomely for privacy's sake would be here in a matter of hours. He just needed an excuse to keep away from Shay and her questions.

The woman was a pit bull. A beautiful, sassy pit bull who should have her hands full with her new boyfriend Leo, instead of trying to ride T.J.'s ass about his divorce.

"Leo and Brute are on the way down," she called from the main area. "They want to speak to you before you leave."

He withheld a sigh and scrubbed both hands down his face. "About?"

"Don't worry, it's nothing intrusive." Her slight frame filled the doorway. "It's business. My business, actually. I came up with a few ideas for the Vault and they want to speak to you privately about it."

Damn it. It was God knows when in the early hours of the morning. He didn't have the brain capacity to think of anything but Cassie. All his mind revolved around were blue eyes, soft curves and a gorgeous smile.

Shay cocked her hip against the door frame. "Can I ask you something?"

No. *Hell no.* He didn't want to talk. Not about work or life. Especially not about love. "I'm tired. Can we do this later?"

"I'm worried about you." Her soft footfalls brushed against the carpet as she strode toward him. "I didn't realize you were stuck in a bad marriage."

"I wasn't stuck." The need to defend Cassie was instantaneous. Painfully so. "It wasn't bad either."

"Then why?" She frowned. "I don't understand."

Neither did Leo or Brute, and that was okay. Their perception of his relationship wasn't important. They were his closest friends, but in contrast, Cassie was his world. The problems that had led to their divorce were private. He wouldn't betray her, even now when they weren't together anymore.

"It's complicated." He bided his time, yanking the fitted sheet off the bed and balling it before launching it toward the pile of cushion covers near the door.

"*That* I can understand. Especially when I assume sexuality played an integral role." She strolled for the bedside table and flicked off the lamp. "But if it wasn't bad, why the divorce?"

"Presuming anything in this lifestyle and working environment is dangerous, Shay." His tone was authoritative. Annoyed. Something he didn't show often. "Misconceptions and thoughtlessness can get you in a lot of trouble." He knew from experience.

"Okay..." She pulled back in offense and strode for the door. "Point taken."

Great. Now, he not only felt like shit, he felt like an asshole, too. "Shay, wait." He jogged after her. "I appreciate your concern, but I'm good. Promise."

She raised a brow and crossed her arms over her chest. "I was only trying to help."

The door from the entry creaked open, burying the conversation. At least he hoped so. The sound of heavy footsteps reached them moments before Leo and Brute strode into the main Vault of Sin room.

"Is this a bad time?" Leo asked, his jaw tight, his gaze locked on Shay.

"No. We're good." Her tone said otherwise as she sidled up to Leo and placed a kiss on his lips. "I'll go upstairs so the three of you can talk." Without another word, she sauntered from the room, closing the door behind her with a harsh clunk.

"Why did she look pissed off?" Leo asked.

"Doesn't she always look like that?" T.J. rested his hip against the side of the tan leather sofa in the middle of the room.

Brute gave a halfhearted snicker. "Yep. She's either pissed or up to something. Neither look is comforting."

"Maybe if you quit giving her hell, she'd quit sharpening her claws." Leo leaned against the back of the sofa. "Just admit you love riling her."

"You know what I'd love?" Brute flashed his teeth in a vicious smile. "I'd love to see you and Shay interact without your dick involved. Get a room. Go on vacation. Just keep your lily-white ass outta my face."

"Jealous much?"

"Fuck y—"

"Come on, guys." T.J. was too tired for this. "Shay said you have something to speak to me about."

Leo smirked, claiming victory over the argument.

"Don't preen like a peacock," Brute demanded. "Now you've gotta explain your crazy girlfriend's fucked-up ideas for our damn sex club."

T.J. closed his eyes, letting exhaustion take hold. He didn't have the strength to participate in this bullshit tonight. He didn't even have the will to smile.

"Relax." Leo nudged his shoulder. "It's not that bad."

Brute cleared his throat. "Depends on your perspective."

"Just spit it out." T.J. scrubbed a hand along his jaw, across the harsh stubble that reminded him he hadn't shaved in two days. "What is Shay up to?"

"She had a few ideas to increase attendance in the Vault."

"The main idea being a dress-up party," Brute drawled.

"What?" T.J. loved Shay, but people dressing up as Fred Flintstone or Superman was not the type of professional image he wanted for their club. Having girlfriends or lovers involved in the decision-making process of their business wasn't something he approved of either. That's why Cassie had always been a silent partner.

"It's a fucking masquerade party, you idiot." Leo shot Brute the bird. "It'll give those who are interested in playing but reluctant to be seen in this type of environment a chance to remain anonymous."

"I'm listening." T.J.'s tiredness abated somewhat. The idea could have merit. Maybe. He jerked his chin in Brute's direction and was immediately pinned by his friend's scowl. "I gather you're against the idea."

"The club has never been about games or *playing* to me. It's a lifestyle choice. Either own up to your proclivities, or fuck off and go to another club—one that doesn't pride itself on integrity and the privacy of all our members."

The reminder of other clubs made cement solidify in T.J.'s gut. He'd been there, done that. It hadn't been pretty. "Just because you're out and proud doesn't mean everyone else has to be. Some of the people interested in the lifestyle aren't willing to risk losing family or friends if they're caught." He knew that all too well. "And others have their religion and employment to think about."

"Don't get me started on religion."

"Or anything else that doesn't gain your approval," Leo muttered.

"So, you *are* against the idea?" T.J. asked. Brute wasn't pro anything. He was the glass-half-empty kind of guy. The one who took pleasure in making others fail. He was brutal, thus the nickname.

"He's fucking fine with it." Leo spoke through a laugh. "He already gave the go-ahead. He's just being his typical moody self."

Brute shrugged. "Your girlfriend is a hard woman to deny."

"*My* girlfriend being the operative words."

It was Brute's turn to chuckle. "Yes, *currently*, she is."

Leo growled and straightened, crossing his arms over his chest.

"Come on, guys." T.J. was going to have to crash on one of the Vault beds if they didn't get this conversation done with. He didn't want to drive to his apartment when he couldn't keep his eyes open. "I guess we all agree about the masquerade party. So where do we go from here?"

Brute laughed. "I'll let Leo answer that one, too."

"Actually..." Leo drew the word out. "Shay's arranged for the first trial run to take place next Thursday night."

T.J. struggled to ignore the nudge of betrayal filling his chest. "Right..." They'd planned it without him.

"We weren't sure when you were going to return to work." Leo held up his hands in surrender. "You've—"

"Doesn't take much to pick up the phone. Or text." He'd never felt more alone. Cassie was gone. The club was moving on without him, evolving, when every part of his soul was crumpling to shit.

"Yeah, well, that's a two-way street." Brute raised an accusatory brow. "You could've given us a heads-up about when you were returning. Or that you planned to bail on us in the first place. This is a business. We rely on you."

Ouch. It wouldn't hurt so much if they weren't right.

"I couldn't deal," he admitted. With work. With the world. With life in general. He'd had no choice. Finding the strength to hand over the divorce papers hadn't been easy. Reflection and determination had taken time.

"We know." Leo nudged his shoulder. "It's no big deal. So, about this masquerade thing..."

"I guess I'll just sit back and let you guys run the show, seeing as you've already started the project." He kept the resentment from his voice the best he could.

Brute smirked. "Don't look at me. This is all on Lothario. He couldn't say no because Shay has his balls in the palm of her hand."

"Shay prefers my balls in her mouth, asshole," Leo snarled. "And to be honest, I always thought it was a good idea. I would've shut her down otherwise."

Brute snorted and received a middle-finger salute in return.

"The entry and dress codes will all remain the same," Leo continued. "We're still obtaining non-disclosures before they arrive, proof of identification and photos. The only difference is that patrons can maintain their anonymity from other guests once they arrive. Brute will know who they are from the online registration."

"Okay." He shrugged. He didn't have the energy to protest even if he did disagree. "Has there been much interest?"

An arrogant smile brightened Leo's features. "We're almost at full capacity."

CHAPTER THREE

*C*assie increased the volume on her earphones, trying to drown out her thoughts. It didn't help that she was sitting at the dining room table, her gaze glued to the website causing the pain in her veins to increase.

Vault of Sin.

She was on their mailing list. Had been since the club opened a year ago. Today, she'd finally had the strength to enter back into the real world—showering, cooking, cleaning the house, and lastly, checking her email.

It was a sign. A blatant nudge from fate. The Vault was holding its first masquerade party. A private, anonymous event. Cassie's heart was racing over the notification. Something churned in her belly, telling her she had to be there. Yeah, it could be indigestion, but she chose to ignore that train of thought.

It was the perfect opportunity to insert herself back into T.J.'s life. Gradually. Without him even knowing. Without *anyone* knowing.

This email acknowledged all her fears and set them at ease. With a disguise, she could attend the event at the Vault and see if T.J. was already moving on. Determine his mindset about the divorce. And hopefully gain a better plan to reconnect. All she had to do was overcome all the obstacles stopping her from getting through the front doors.

She'd never stepped foot in the private part of the business. No matter how intrigued she was by the mere thought of her husband's sex club, there hadn't been time to visit. Not since her relationship with T.J. had hit rocky ground around the same time the establishment had opened. Beforehand, he'd spoken to her at length about his involvement, obtaining her understanding over the duties he would be required to perform. She'd trusted him. Unequivocally. The only unmanageable emotion she had felt had been excitement, knowing the club would eventually become a part of their sexual journey.

That part of their future had never eventuated.

Now, the place readily available for sex and seduction was constantly on her mind. Not only because it was a significant threat to losing her husband to another woman, it was also the perfect location to try and win him back.

"Cassie," a female voice called behind her, followed by a loud knock that startled her to her feet, the earplugs painfully yanking from her ears as her chair fell to the floor.

"It's just me." Jan, her friend from across the street, held up her hands from the other side of the glass sliding door. "I didn't mean to scare you."

"Well, you failed miserably." Cassie breathed deeply, working hard to calm the rapid beat of her heart. Six months hadn't been enough time to get used to living without a man in the house. She still found it hard sleeping alone, without T.J. to protect her.

Obviously, Bear wasn't the best guard dog either. He currently sat at Jan's side, his large tail wagging, his eyes bright with playfulness.

Cassie unlocked the door and slid it open. "What are you doing here?" *Again.*

Jan shrugged. "Just dropping by before I hit the sack."

"I've told you—" *a hundred times*, "—that isn't necessary. I swear, I'm fine." Or she would be. One day. In the unforeseeable future. Depending on the outcome of her marriage.

"Sweetie, you lost your husband."

"I didn't *lose* him." She knew exactly where he was. "He's just stubborn, that's all. He'll be back before you know it."

Jan gave her a placating smile. "Are you sure? He doesn't seem the type of man to make mistakes. Especially big ones."

There was a first for everything. T.J. was a man that owned everything he did—his attitude, his strength, his determination. Most importantly, his love for her. He just hid his confidence under a gentlemanly façade, not needing to prove himself to anyone. It was only a matter of time before she convinced him to return. But there was no point arguing with Jan. She would never understand. Nobody would.

Jan's gaze drifted to Cassie's laptop screen, her brow furrowing. "What are you looking at?"

Oh, Christ. Cassie lunged toward the laptop and slammed the screen closed to cut off the sordid images that set the scene on the Vault's website. "Nothing."

Jan's lip twitched. "Did I interrupt something?"

"*No.* Of course not."

"You sure you weren't watching porn?" Jan raised a brow. "Did I fuck with your motion of the ocean?"

"Oh, my God." Heat burned in her cheeks. "No." The last thing her body was capable of was arousal.

"So, what were you looking at?"

"Nothing."

Jan cocked her hip, settling into a comfortable position

that wordlessly announced she wasn't going anywhere without an answer.

"Fine." Cassie huffed and crossed her arms over her chest. "I'm working out a plan to get T.J. back."

"With the help of porn?" Jan's expression turned bleak.

"It's not *goddamn* porn."

"Okay, okay." Jan balked. "Then explain."

Cassie didn't want to. There were things in life that should be kept between husband and wife. Their reason for divorce was one of them. So was the plan for trying to get him back. Even though Jan was older and more open-minded than the friends Cassie had grown up with, it still didn't seem like a conversation they should be having. "I can't. It would feel like I was betraying him."

"Cass..." Jan pulled out a chair and took a seat. "You don't owe him anything. He already wants to move on."

Damn. The truth stung. "There's other reasons, too."

"Like?"

"Like I don't want you to judge him. Or us as a couple. Our relationship wasn't normal by society's standards."

"Right..." Jan raised a haughty brow. "I'm going to pretend I'm not offended by your assumption, and remind you I'm a single forty-two-year-old that has never had a prudish bone in my body."

Although Jan had become her closest confidant in the months since T.J. had moved out, Cassie hadn't shared private information. Only heartache and fear for the future. The secrets she kept with her husband were a gift only the two of them shared. They'd never been the type to crave attention. T.J. guarded the intimate parts of his life. They both did. He'd learned through the mistakes of his friends that people were too quick to judge decisions that were none of their business.

"If you can't tell me—" Jan reached for the laptop, "—show me what you were looking at."

Cassie warred with herself, caught between needing to talk and having to remain true to her husband. She still didn't believe T.J. wanted to move on. She could change his mind. She knew she could. It was loneliness that pushed her to share her pain.

"Please keep an open mind." She spared her friend a brief glance before she lifted the laptop screen and swiped her fingers over the mouse pad. The Vault website burst to life as Jan scooted closer in her chair.

"What am I looking at?"

The inside of Cassie's wildest fantasies. "An invitation to a sex club."

Jan's eyes widened as she began to nod, slowly, not taking her focus from the page before her.

"T.J. is going to be there." At least she thought he would be. His name adorned the bottom of the invitation after all.

"He's been cheating on you?" Jan screeched. She glanced over her shoulder, her face a mask of fury. "He told you that?"

"No." Cassie shook her head, clutching the back of the wooden chair in front of her. "It's not like that. He's not there to have sex." As far as she knew. "This club is part of the business he owns with his friends. Very few people know of its existence."

"Right." Jan chuckled, the sound almost delirious. "I guess it's true—the quiet ones are always the freakiest in the sack."

Cassie gave a halfhearted smile. "He was definitely talented in that department."

"So how does this club work in with winning him back? Or can't you tell me that either?"

Cassie sagged under the weight of hopelessness. She hadn't told anyone the real reason T.J. had asked for a divorce. Not even the blatant lie of *incompatibility* stated on the legal documentation. It was too private. Being vague was her only option.

"T.J. isn't like most guys. He cherished me. He was a protector. A provider—in every sense of the word. He continuously worked at maintaining our perfect marriage and prided himself on his dedication to me."

"He placed you on a pedestal."

Exactly. "Yes. He did that, too. His love was infallible."

"But?"

Cassie sighed. "He placed too much onus on his responsibility in our relationship. It was almost an obsession to keep me happy, and I completely adored the attention. If I was sick, he nurtured me to health. If I was sad, he figured out a way to brighten my mood. My contentment was everything to him."

"Until?"

Cassie shrugged. "Everything went to hell a year ago. I placed myself in a bad position. A *really* bad position. I was hurt, and he blames himself. He always blames himself."

Jan shook her head with a disbelieving furrow of her brow. "How come you never told me any of this?"

"The circumstances aren't..." Socially acceptable? Morally adequate? "Favorable."

"Okay, I get that you want to keep the details close to your chest. So, let's return the convo to the fuck club. What's that got to do with getting him back?"

Fuck club?

Cassie smiled. "We've been emotionally disconnected for twelve months. I want to get to know him again—his strengths and weaknesses. I need to be close to him, maybe then things will be clearer."

"Then go. Do it. Get your kink on, you naughty little girl."

Cassie couldn't contain her laugh. "It's not that easy. Although the night in question will be their first masquerade party, there's a line of hoops I need to jump

31

through to gain entry. One of them being proof of identification."

"And..."

"And I know the person who handles applications. If he sees my name, he won't let me in." Brute was a hard-ass. A man who couldn't be swayed or easily fooled.

"So, what you're saying is that you need a new identity?"

"What I need is a new name, face, body—everything." It was useless. Cassie leaned over the back of the chair and scrolled to the page on the Vault of Sin website which listed entry requirements. "There." She pointed to the screen. "I need a recent photo, plus a copy of my driver's license."

"Is that all?" Jan focused on the website, her eyes squinted.

Is that all? "I don't think you understand. I can't get in with my current license. They'll recognize me straightaway."

"What if you used someone else's? Maybe someone that looks similar to you."

"No." Cassie shook her head. "That would mean telling more people, and that's not something I'm willing to do."

"We need a fake ID."

"Yeah," Cassie spoke with derision. In her reality, obtaining illegal documents was as likely as robbing a bank. "I'll just ask one of the criminal mastermind friends of mine to whip one up for me."

"Don't give me sass, girlie. I'm sure we can sort something out."

The dull beat of Cassie's heart began to thud with earnest. The slightest glimmer of hope sparked a fire under her ribs. "We can?"

"Yeah. Maybe. I dunno." Jan turned to face her. "I can give you a makeover. We'll concentrate on being the opposite of how you are now—fake nails, salon tan, bright makeup, ostentatious clothes. And with the right wig, you could look completely different."

"It still leaves the problem of identification." Fooling Brute wouldn't be easy, yet her appearance was the least difficult part of the plan.

"That's where my brother may be able to help." Jan pushed from her seat. "You may not know any criminal masterminds, but I'm sure he does."

"Isn't he a cop?" Cassie closed her gaping mouth. This was crazy. "I don't want to get arrested."

Jan waved her comment away. "You'll be fine. As long as you still want to go ahead with your plan."

Shady police. Lies. Illegal activity. Was it worth it? "Yes. I do."

"Then leave it to me. How much time do I have?"

"Four days until the party, but I need to submit my application as soon as possible."

Jan winced. "Okay. First thing tomorrow, you need to get to work on changing your appearance. Leave the ID to me."

Christ. This was really happening. She was going to walk into an unfamiliar sex club, dressed in a disguise, and try to win back her husband. She was even prepared to break the law. *Ha.* The level of devotion was crazy. But for T.J., it was all worth it.

CHAPTER FOUR

*T*he days leading to the fateful night were a whirlwind. Cassie didn't sleep, barely ate and her boss didn't cut her any slack when he found out about the impending divorce. Not that she'd expected him to. The dictator of the hotel she worked at was a ballbuster who didn't hide his disapproval over her new fake tan and plum polish highlighting longer-than-normal nails.

"This is the driveway, right?" Jan asked from the driver's seat.

"Yeah, go through to the parking lot out back." They slowly glided past the large building with impeccably clean windows giving a look into the interior of Taste of Sin. Beside the door to the restaurant was the darkened entry to Shot of Sin. It was currently abandoned. The dance club wasn't open on Thursday nights.

"Are you ready?"

Nope. "Yes." Cassie's voice was filled with panic, her heart a rampant beat in her chest.

The twenty-minute journey to T.J.'s business had been done in nerve-filled silence. She had no clue what would happen once she arrived. She didn't even know if she'd get inside. After submitting her application, she was sure a rejection would soon follow. She'd even stalked her email, unsure if it would be better emotionally to gain approval to see her husband, or take it as a sign if her request was denied.

Days had gone by and she still didn't know if this was the right idea.

Jan pulled into one of the parking spaces at the back of Shot of Sin and cut the ignition. "Now, remember, call me at any time to come pick you up. I'll be waiting."

Oh, Christ. This was really happening.

"Stop fretting." Jan placed a hand on Cassie's shoulder and squeezed. "No man is going to want to squish your titties when you look like you're about to vomit."

"I'm not going to vomit." Her conviction was a lie. She was light-headed. Scared. And she wasn't sure what worried her most—entering a sex club she wasn't familiar with or the possibility of finding another woman in her husband's arms.

"I'm just not sure if I can do this." The admission was painful. As if she were giving up. Admitting defeat.

"No problem. I'll drive us home." Jan started the ignition.

"*Wait.*" Damn it. "You and your damn reverse psychology."

Jan smirked. "It worked, didn't it?"

Cassie growled and fought the need to scratch under the wig itching her scalp. "You're so mean to me." She grasped for her handbag and unclicked her seat belt. "I need a few minutes to prepare."

Jan rolled her eyes. "You already said that when I wanted to get started on your hair. Then again when I attempted to do your makeup. *And* when I tried to get you in the car. Not to mention the three laps around the block you made me do."

"I'm walking into a sex club, not a Seven-Eleven."

"Your husband is down there. You'll be fine."

"I *think* my husband is down there." Cassie shoved the car door open with force. "I have no confirmation of that."

"Then think of it as an adventure. Even if you don't participate, you're about to see more action than I have in years."

Cassie grabbed her clutch and shoved from the car. "Still not comforting."

"Don't forget about your mask," Jan cooed. "I love you, you naughty little minx."

Still hidden behind the car, Cassie pulled her mask into place. "Thanks," she drawled and closed the door on her friend's laughter.

As Jan's car drove from the parking lot, Cassie began to shake. She was on her own. Vulnerable. Looking like a whore and feeling like a clown in all her fake attire. The dark blue dress sculpting her curves was unlike anything she'd usually wear. It was tight. Too tight. And it was only there to save her thinly veiled modesty during the short walk to the back entrance of the sex club. Once inside, she would need to remove it and reveal the skimpy slip she wore underneath to fit the clubs scantily clad dress code.

Everything adorning her body was new, and the exact opposite of what she would normally wear. Her shiny heels were stiletto thin, the color perfectly matching the dark purple of her nails and the lace outlining her mask. There was no turning back. Not unless she wanted to strut her hooker-heels to the curb and call Jan to pick her up.

She glanced toward the back entrance of the club, to the couple standing at the door getting their ID checked by two men. They were tall, broad, burly males who seemed ominous under the dim glow of the outside light yards above their heads.

Their faces came into focus as she approached, her footsteps crunching against the asphalt. One guard was dressed in navy slacks and a white-collared shirt. His expression was friendly, comforting. The man beside him was not. His stare was lethal, his features tight as he scrutinized the people before him. Typical Brute. She'd never forget his critical stare, the one that hid the caring man underneath. Deep, deep underneath. His gaze wasn't even upon her, yet she already felt the weight of it. Grueling, criticizing. *Shit.* She shouldn't be doing this.

He was going to recognize her no matter how she'd tried to hide her identity. Her long blonde hair was now short and black, thanks to the excessively itchy wig. Her light blue eyes were dark brown from the contacts she'd purchased from her optometrist. And her lips, usually adorned with gentle colors, were bright red and glossy, standing out like a beacon in the dead of night. The only solace she gained was from the mask that covered most of her forehead, the area around her eyes and down to her cheek bones, giving her a sense of anonymity.

What if she had to take it off to prove her identity?

Hell. Heart in her throat, she came to stand at the end of the line and smiled at the woman who turned to greet her with a flash of perfect teeth. The bright pink mask she wore was covered in glitter with some of the shimmering glow resting on her cheeks.

"This your first time?" The woman's gaze fell to the red band around Cassie's wrist.

"Yes." Her voice faltered, not only from nerves. She couldn't fail at this. Brute couldn't turn her away. She wouldn't know what to do if he did.

"You'll have fun, I promise." The woman turned to her companion and stepped forward, offering Brute their identification.

Cassie's throat tightened. Blood rushed through her ears in a painful thrum she was sure the whole world could hear.

Then the couple disappeared, moving forward, out of sight, leaving her to stand face-to-face with Brute, his hand outstretched as she convinced herself not to run.

"ID," he grunted.

She placed her fake driver's license in his hand and hoped he didn't notice the tremor in her fingers. She was sweating. The back of her neck tingled. Her scalp itched.

"Name?" he muttered.

Oh, no. He already had her identification. Her name was clearly written on it. He was testing her.

"Tanya Johnson." Her voice broke. This wouldn't work. Not in her meek, frightened state of mind. She had to place this in perspective. Her marriage was on the line. Her happiness. Everything that had ever mattered to her was dependent on reconnecting with T.J.

She raised her chin, cleared her throat and met Brute's stare as he palmed a small electronic tablet in his hand.

"First-timer." His gaze lowered over her chest, her stomach, then came to rest on her arm. "Make sure you don't remove the wristband."

"I won't."

He grunted, making her increasingly aware he hadn't outgrown his arrogant attitude in the months since she'd seen him last.

"We have strict rules here, Tanya."

"I know."

Brute's position at the entry was deliberate. Not only to check identification, but to give an unspoken warning to everyone who passed through the doors. If word got out about Vault of Sin, he would deal with it. Harshly. He was the brutality protecting the carnal pleasure beneath the Shot of Sin dance floor.

"Be sure to adhere to them and you'll have a great time." His lethal tone implied otherwise. "If you have any problems or concerns, there's staff members dressed in full attire to help you—Leo, T.J. and Travis."

The sound of her husband's name sent a barb of fire through her chest. He was here. In a sex club. No longer needing to remain a voyeur as he would soon be single.

"And if you'd prefer to discuss any issues with a female member of staff," Brute continued, "let me know and I'll arrange it."

She inclined her head and broke eye contact, unable to hold his lethal stare. "Thank you."

He moved to the side, allowing her stomach to drop to the tips of her toes as she started forward into the darkness. A cement staircase came into view, the couple before her barely visible as they reached the bottom landing and turned left.

She focused on the path before her, trying not to let past experience taint this moment. T.J. would never align himself with sleaziness. She had to trust her memory of him. She had to trust the Vault of Sin. It was a mantra. A comforting acknowledgement she had to repeat over and over again to keep her feet progressing to the start of the stairs.

"Oh, boy." Dizzying nerves, stiletto heels and a rapid descent. Not a great combination.

The sound of sex, chatter and clinking glassware entered her ears as she progressed at a snail's pace, not allowing nausea to creep in.

"You'll be fine," a female voice spoke over her shoulder.

Cassie reached out a hand to grip the wall. She glanced behind her to the smile almost covered by the green feathers bordering the blonde's mask, the color almost perfectly matching her eyes.

"Don't panic." The woman's gaze lowered, her lips curving sweetly when she spied the red band adorning Cassie's wrist.

"The first time is always the worst. Just stay away from the bukkake ritual."

Holy shit. Was she serious?

"I'm joking. I'm joking." The woman chuckled and grabbed the crook of Cassie's elbow. "I should know better than to tease."

"It's okay," Cassie croaked. Sure it was. She just couldn't get the image of a group of men poised over her kneeling body as they prepared to spray her face with their release. *Shudder.* "I'm a little nervous, that's all." And apprehensive. And nauseous. And scared.

"You came alone?"

They began to descend together, the woman's gentle touch still resting on Cassie's arm. "Yeah. Stupid, right?"

"Not at all. My first Vault experience was on my own."

Cassie's concern began to ebb under the woman's comforting voice. There was no sexual inclination to her touch. Cassie's intuition told her to trust this woman. To believe her friendship was genuine. Then again, her intuition had been nowhere in sight for the last twelve months, so what the hell did she know?

They reached the bottom step and the calming grip on her arm disappeared. The sound of sex and excited conversation had grown. Loud enough to ring in her ears. With trepidation, she turned on the tips of her sexy shoes and came face-to-face with her first glimpse of the Vault of Sin.

"*Holy smokes.*" Her words were a whispered breath.

She could only see the corner of what she assumed was a large room. And in that corner was a sex swing. An *occupied* sex swing. The woman was reclined on her back, her torso encased in black straps, her legs wrapped around a Greek god as he sank into her. Over and over again. Her dark hair hung in the air behind her, the glossy strands swaying with each thrust.

It was glorious. Stupefying in its perfection. They paid no attention to her fascination, or the other people within view who were also watching. It was as if they were alone. Immersed in their own bubble of pleasure.

"Are swings your thing?" The woman beside her asked.

Cassie shook her head, still unable to drag her focus away from the live porn before her. "I've never tried one."

"Tonight might be your lucky night."

Cassie coughed to smother a laugh. "No. Not tonight."

There would be no sex for her, even though the tingle of arousal was already pulsing between her thighs. This was about getting to know T.J. again. Finding out where he was at. What he was thinking. Maybe she would reveal herself to him, maybe she wouldn't. But sex wasn't in the equation as far as she was concerned.

"You never know." The woman chuckled. "I'm Zoe by the way."

"Cas—" *Shit.* Cassie snapped her attention from the fornicating couple and pasted on a fake smile. "I'm Tanya."

Zoe's smile faltered, suspicion growing heavy in the narrowing of her framed eyes. "Come on, Tanya. I'll escort you to the change rooms."

Cassie wasn't sure if her slip up had been a close call or the other woman had no curiosity to pry. Either way, she released a silent sigh of relief. Zoe strode from the darkened hall, her shoulders back, her head high with grace and dignity. Cassie tried to mimic the confidence, failing miserably with the awe assailing her as the full room came into view.

A crowd of people mingled along a long stretch of bar. They were all in different stages of undress. Some women were in corsets, others in bras and panties. A few were

topless. The men on the other hand were in boxer briefs—
Calvin Klein, Emporio Armani, Tommy John.

The area screamed with invigorating debauchery. There
were chaises, a bed, maybe more than one. She couldn't see
much over the people constricting her view. Two doors were
open to her left, with the shadows of people inside. And an
archway was to the far end of the room.

It was different from what she'd experienced in the only
other club she'd been to. The ambiance, although dripping
with seduction, was classy. Everything was red and black—
sheets, lamp shades, furniture.

The people surrounding her were young, fit and
attractive. Complete contrasts to the old, overweight men
who'd lined the walls of the previous club she'd run from. She
turned in a circle, amazed and more than a little proud at the
perfection of the atmosphere.

"It's this way." Zoe raised her voice and didn't
acknowledge the loud cry of, "Oh yes, oh yes, fuck me
harder," from the woman in the sex swing.

"I'm right behind you." She was following, no matter how
stunted her steps.

Curiosity had her enthralled, but there was something
that began to concern her. She'd memorized every inch of the
main room, taken a glimpse into the two private areas, and
not once had she caught sight of her husband.

~

"*A*re you coming down to the party?"

T.J. squeezed his eyes shut and massaged his
lids, ignoring the question for as long as he could. Shay
wouldn't leave him alone. She hovered. Everywhere. All the
time. No matter where he went, she was in his tracks with a
friendly smile and a comforting pat on his back. He loathed

it. The old Shay, the one who'd talked smack and given him hell, was the woman he needed. Not this highly attuned, feminine ball of emotional support that kept him on edge.

"I'll get down there when I'm ready." The growl of his voice echoed through the empty Shot of Sin dance club. He liked the peace and quiet. And he deserved the loneliness.

"Did you think about what I said in the restaurant yesterday?"

He couldn't forget. Shay's idea of getting over his wife was to move on. Hop on the bike again, so to speak. Take a new woman for a test drive. Brute concurred, ever the heartless bastard.

The thought made him sick.

"Why don't we talk about you for a change?" He dropped his hand from his face and straightened at the sight of her. She was adorned in a see-through black dress, her shiny red bra and panties visible beneath to match her glossy high heels. She wore a swatch of black lace over her eyes. Simple yet elegant. *Beautiful.*

"How are things with you and Leo?" He spoke to hide his discomfort. Seeing Shay like this wasn't something he could get used to overnight. She'd been his friend for a long time. His employee even longer. Now he'd have to watch as she strutted her gorgeous body around the Vault on her nights off.

She rolled her pretty brown eyes. "You know, you could just tell me you don't want to talk."

Perfect. "I don't want to talk about it, Shayna." His glare was far harsher than his tone. He couldn't help it. He was tired—his heart, his body and his mind. Enough was enough.

"No problem." She raised her chin, the defiance of the woman he used to know coming back in full force.

"So how about you and Leo? What did I miss while I was away?"

She waggled her brows. "A lot of debauchery."

No way. Leo was taking it slow, unwilling to risk scaring her away from the lifestyle. "Are you fucking with me?"

"Yes." Her smile was bright. "We're taking our relationship day by day."

"But you're enjoying yourself." He could see it in the undiluted happiness of her features. She was no longer opposed to the Vault. The realization stung. Why couldn't it have turned out this way for him and Cass? Why did he have to ruin what they could've been?

Because he couldn't help fucking up.

"I'm glad the two of you are working things out." He hadn't been able to do the same with his wife. The guilt was too heavy, the weight of regret a constant punishment. Everything else that followed was like an avalanche burying the happiness he'd once had. "I suppose I better get downstairs and show Leo and Brute I'm not slacking off."

He pushed from the stool and strode to her. "I hope you're right about this masquerade party."

She flashed him a confident smile. "I am."

He followed her down the stairs to the Vault. They passed people in the hall, couples, singles, some dressed in evening attire, others already in lingerie and making their way back into the main part of the club. All of them wore masks to partially or completely hide their faces.

"Hey, Zoe," Shay called out.

Zoe James, one of their regulars, sauntered toward them. "I'm loving this masquerade idea."

She wore a flattering shimmery dress, her sexy attire matching her equally appealing personality. However, it was her companion, the dark-haired woman lingering behind her, that caught his attention.

Her inability to hold his gaze confirmed her club virginity before his focus had a chance to rest on her wristband. The poor woman was distraught, her wringing hands another indication of her anxiety.

If it were any other day, maybe he would've tried to offer support. A welcoming smile or an indication for Shay to show her around. But there was something about her that put him on edge. She was *too* nervous, her gaze lowering almost as if in submission as he scrutinized her.

Did he know her? Something inside him sparked familiarity, yet he couldn't place her features. He usually noticed the blondes. Ones who didn't need to bolster their confidence behind a mask of bright lipstick and dark eye makeup. This woman was a poser. The type to boost her esteem through a fake façade.

So why was he suddenly comparing her features to his wife? *Fuck.* He needed to ditch the matrimonial titles and remember Cassie was destined to be his ex.

A new wave of hurt hit him as he tore his gaze away and massaged his forehead to fight the lingering thoughts. "I gotta get going." He maneuvered around them, not chancing another glance at the woman. "I'll see you all inside."

This was what it had been like all week. All month. Every woman reminded him of Cassie. Every shadow was hers. She was already haunting him, and there was nothing he could do about it. Not that he wanted to rid himself of her presence. The memories, although painful, were also a blessing. Without her, he was nothing.

He entered a four-digit code into the panel at the closed door at the end of the hall and yanked the heavy wood open. Pleasure bombarded him. Not his own, unfortunately. The fulfillment of others surrounded him as he strode through the newbie area and into the main room of Vault of Sin.

He inclined his head at guests, recognizing some and completely oblivious to the identity of others as he maneuvered around patrons. Beds were already in use, their occupants participating in varying degrees of flirtation, foreplay and sex.

Leo was behind the bar, dressed the same as T.J. in a suit and tie—standard attire for Vault staff.

Leo jerked his head in greeting. "I'm glad you came."

"Was there ever any doubt?"

He hated the diminished respect Leo and Brute had tried to hide due to his time off. Since returning, they tiptoed around him, treating him like a casual part of the ownership team instead of an equal partner.

"Maybe a little."

T.J. winced. "Well, I'm here. What do you need me to do?"

"Want to take over helping Travis while I do a walk-around? Brute will be finished assisting security at the door soon. Then I think the two of us should relax and take the night off." A smirk curled the corner of Leo's lips. "You never know, you might find someone willing to occupy your time."

"Yeah, whatever." He ignored yet another hint to move on from his wife. *His ex.* He'd never get used to calling Cassie that.

They didn't understand. If you fell off a bike and skinned your knee, you got straight back on to fight the childish fear. If you shattered your marriage, devastating not only your own life, but also the future of the one person who would forever hold your heart, you didn't slide straight back into the dating pool. You waited for the burn to heal. You waited for the shattered parts of your soul to return from wherever the fuck they'd fled to, so you could finally sleep at night and gain some perspective that wasn't tarnished by the psychotic ramblings of insomnia.

Or maybe you didn't. Maybe you cut and run. How the hell did he know? Was it best to take a shot of cement, harden the hell up and build that damn bridge straightaway?

Fuck. Nothing made sense. Nothing mattered. There was no longer a paved road toward the perfect future.

He was in limbo.

In the past, sex had always had healing qualities. The rush of release, the boost of endorphins. Hooking up with a random woman and starting the transition could be the best thing for him.

Doubtful.

He was so damn sick of the confusion. The warring emotions. It was bad enough making the decision to leave Cassie in the first place. Moving on seemed harder. Permanent. A divorce only ruined the piece of paper that made them husband and wife. Sleeping with someone else would finalize the process. Never to be rekindled.

He needed to sort his shit out. Now. Before he lost any more respect and entitlement.

So, who was he? The bastard in need of closure? Or the man who'd vowed to forever remain true to Cassie, even after divorce tore them apart?

Hell. He didn't have a clue, but by the end of the night, he had a feeling he would.

CHAPTER FIVE

*W*ith shaky hands, Cassie placed her dress in the locker. Her skin was still on fire from the run-in with T.J. in the hall. It may be delusional or wishful thinking, but she could've sworn there'd been a spark of recognition in his eyes. Pain, too.

"Are you meeting anyone here tonight?" Zoe asked. "Maybe your husband..."

Cassie looked down at herself, making sure her slip covered all her important parts. Her breasts had barely fit into the cups, their volume overflowing and creating a mass of cleavage. She didn't have the courage to expose her stomach. The vulnerability of showing her thighs was hard enough with the material barely reaching the bottom of her matching panties. The more skin she covered, the better—for her confidence and T.J.'s inability to recognize her.

"I'm not married." Cassie closed the locker door. She didn't want to go into the details of her failed love life. The less connection she had to T.J., the smaller the chance of getting caught.

Zoe raised her chin and focused on Cassie's hands. "Your rings say otherwise."

"Oh, *shit*." She turned her body away, frantically working the jewelry from her wedding finger. "It's not what you think."

The room filled with silence, the comforting aura Zoe had bathed her in washed away. Cassie worked the rings off and hastened to enter the security pin into the electronic locker keypad before anyone else spied the telling jewelry. "I'm not married," she blurted. "Or I soon won't be."

How could she have forgotten her rings? They'd been a constant symbol of love and affection, more so since T.J. had abandoned her. They were the lifeline she gazed upon for fortitude. One glimpse at the diamonds adorning her finger would've been enough for her husband to recognize her.

"It's not my business." Zoe's voice was low. "If cheating is your thing, so be it. I just think you should know that you'll be booted if the owners find out. They don't need the drama that will arise from a jealous lover."

Cassie closed the locker door again, keeping her palm against the cool metal. "Please..." She didn't know what to ask for. Help? Privacy? A hug? "My husband is meant to be here."

There was no reason to trust this woman. None other than instinct. Yet, Cassie did anyway. There was something in the woman's demeanor. The way she held her head high, her shoulders straight, with comfort shining bright in her eyes.

"My husband *is* here," Cassie repeated, stronger this time. "He wants a divorce, and I'm here to win him back."

Silence.

They were alone in the room, the chattering voices from people in the hall echoing from outside. Cassie glanced to the side and met Zoe's gaze. There was no longer friendship in her features. There was concern. Uncertainty... Pity.

"Do you need help?" she asked, although the pained tone announced she was out of her depth.

"No." Cassie straightened. "All I need is a minute to myself to figure out what the hell I'm doing before I go in there."

Zoe nodded, her brief glimpse of skin above her mask announcing her frown. "If you need someone, please find me. I'm usually in the first private room closest to the parking-lot entrance."

Cassie gave a halfhearted smile in thanks. She was doing this all wrong. She wanted to show T.J. she was strong. Capable. For him, she could be fearless, facing the pain of the past, all for him. *Them.*

Zoe sauntered toward the door and paused inside the frame. "Make sure you find me if you need me." Then she was gone, allowing silence to sink back into the small space.

Cassie rested her back on the locker and let her head clang against the metal. What was she doing? She was half-dressed, in a sex club, hiding under a disguise in an attempt to...what? She could be a voyeur and merely watch to see if he was moving on. Or maybe seduce him, proving he was drawn to her even when her identity was cloaked.

Butterflies crept into her stomach, growing with every second she remained immobile. There'd been nothing to lose by entering the Vault. Apart from her dignity, and that was currently veiled. Nobody needed to know of her desperation to win T.J. back. She needed to stop succumbing to nerves and get this over and done with. She was running out of time and didn't have the luxury to second-guess herself.

She pushed from the lockers and strode for the door. She followed after another couple, thankful they'd remembered the code to get into the main part of the club because she couldn't remember the digits she'd been assigned in her approval letter.

Inside, there were more people than earlier. She passed two softly murmuring couples in the newbie lounge, their conversation unhindered by the large screen of porn playing beside them.

Her scalp itched as she dawdled through the rooms, getting to know her surroundings. People greeted her with smiles, others didn't notice her existence because they were balls-deep in pussy or throat-deep in cock.

One of the private rooms contained numerous pieces of furniture. Almost like a maze of chaises, ottomans and silk-lined single mattresses. Most of which were occupied. There was a mass of mingling bodies, all of them glistening with the slight sheen of pleasure-induced sweat.

The second room was where she found Zoe, caught between two gorgeous men on the bed, aglow from lights in the ceiling. Both males were naked and paying homage to the woman's lingerie-covered body, their attention transfixed. It was another exquisite scene where adoration played a vital role. There was no cockiness. No superiority. The three of them admired one another in scrapes of teeth and gentle swipes of fingers.

"Beautiful, isn't it?"

Cassie glanced over her shoulder to the woman who had greeted Zoe when they'd first arrived—Shay—an employee her husband had spoken about many times.

"Very beautiful." Cassie turned her attention to the main room to shield her face. "In fact, they've made me quite thirsty. Please excuse me while I get a drink."

"No problem."

Cassie walked away, discretely eying T.J.'s employee as she placed distance between them. Sometimes women were more perceptive than men. She didn't want to risk Shay sensing her apprehension and informing management. At least not before she had a chance to speak to her husband.

She entered the main area and came to a halt at the bar, her heart kicking up in pace at the man who sat at the far end. The short wisps of his brown hair hung around his forehead as he sipped from the scotch glass in his hand. He was more familiar than her own body. His image more necessary to her senses than the need to breathe.

From the side, he seemed gaunt. Defeated. The desire to soothe him was painful. But at least he wasn't happy, she supposed. His acceptance of their separation would've hurt more.

She drifted toward him, her feet moving of their own accord, her gaze glued to his frame. The stool beside him was taken, the man in her periphery barely visible because her vision was only attuned to one person. Had only ever been.

"Would you like a seat?" The guy beside T.J. stood, his hand gently clutching hers to guide her forward.

"Thank you." She didn't divert her attention from her husband.

She was so close. Their arms would almost touch if she placed them on the bar. That's all it would take, a brush of skin, a graze of appreciation. He was lost. So was she. But they were side by side and could find their way home together. All she had to do was open her mouth. Start a conversation. Give him hope and love.

She leaned in, her chest pounding the closer she moved, the more potent the scent of his deep, woody aftershave became. Her throat tightened. Memories of the past assailed her. She loved this man so much. It wasn't the typical love found between a man and woman—the jovial smiles and regularly scheduled affection. They were much more than that. Their relationship had been a constant barrage of devotion. Each day growing more intense than the last. Every memory was bathed in happiness that would never be tainted.

She breathed deep of his aftershave, gaining strength from the well-known scent.

"Hi," she murmured.

CHAPTER SIX

T.J. sipped his scotch, unable to lift his game to help out with his own business.

He should be greeting guests, making them feel welcome and at home. Especially when there were more newbies than usual tonight. The party was a success. He just couldn't bring himself to be happy about the influx of fresh patrons.

He missed Cassie. All the more now because he knew it was over. The divorce was in motion, unable to be stopped. At least not by her.

"Hi."

He straightened at the sound of her voice and snapped his gaze to the woman settled on the stool beside him. *Fuck.* The delusions had returned. Not in a vision this time, but her tone.

"Did I startle you?" She edged back, apprehension filling her brown eyes.

"No." His voice was gruff. Unforgiving. "You just sound like someone I know."

Her ruby lips parted, working up and down in a blatant show of unease. What the hell was he thinking? The woman was nothing like his wife. The eyes, framed by a concealing mask, were dark, not the inviting shade of light blue he'd fallen in love with. She had a short, black bob haircut instead of the long locks he'd adored tangling his fingers in. Fuck-me lips that resembled those of his wife, but Cassie's mouth had always been soft and sweet with warm inviting shades, instead of tawdry colors.

"I'm sorry." He focused back on his drink. "I didn't mean to be rude."

The woman cleared her throat. "It's okay."

Her voice was different now, sultrier. Nothing like Cassie's voice. It merely proved his insanity. He needed to move on. To focus on something other than the perfect gift he'd thrown away.

"Do you want a drink?" It was a lame attempt at an apology, but it was the best he could do under the circumstances.

"I'd love one."

"What can I get you?"

"Umm..."

He glanced at her from the corner of his eye. She was biting her lip in an excruciatingly familiar way. He couldn't stop seeing his wife reflected back at him, the way her teeth worked in deep concentration. He needed to get a grip.

"Malibu and lemonade, please."

She met his gaze and her fake eyelashes flickered in an alluring message he chose to ignore.

"Travis?" He jutted his chin at the bartender and waited for the man's attention. "Malibu and lemonade for the lady, and another scotch for me."

"Sure thing." Travis began fixing their order.

"Where's your mask?" the woman uttered. "And why are you still dressed?"

"I'm working." He fought to curb the agitation in his

tone. It wasn't her fault he was losing his mind. If someone with completely opposite features to his wife was driving him crazy with recognition, he needed help.

"Doesn't look like it to me."

He followed her gaze to the fresh glass Travis slid into his hand. No, it didn't look like it to him either. But he wouldn't be able to move until he overcame the ache in his chest. Another drink would do it. Maybe two.

"I'm taking a short break."

She smiled, stealing the air from his lungs with her beauty. *Fuck*. What the hell was happening to him? She was his wife. His fantasy. The same bone structure, the same body frame. Yet, everything else didn't align.

"Is this your first time?" *Shit*. He already knew the answer. He'd seen her wristband earlier when she'd been with Zoe.

"Yeah." She raised her arm and showed the red plastic strip around her wrist. "First time here, but not to this type of establishment."

Right. He needed to quit this conversation and put a stop to the hallucinations. His interest in the woman was a betrayal to his marriage—a marriage that would soon be over. He stared straight ahead, his gaze forsaking his brain to go in search of her reflection in the mirror behind the bar. He couldn't look away. There was something about her. Something he recognized yet couldn't put his finger on.

"Would you mind showing me around?"

There was more than one question in her gravel-rich words. But could he take her up on it? Even for a brief moment to innocently show her around?

"Please." She met his stare in the mirror, her sultry lips tilting at the sides. "It's all a bit daunting."

His heart thumped in his chest, and he wasn't sure if it was from apprehension or anticipation. Without thought, he was on his feet, his body moving of its own volition. She was teasing him. Seducing him. And he was powerless under her spell...or maybe his heart just yearned for something other than alcohol to occupy his mind.

She wasn't his type, that was for sure. He'd always preferred blondes. Women that didn't rely on fake nails and the slightly unnatural glow of a salon tan to boost their appeal. She may remind him of Cassie, yet his dick remained true to his wife.

He outstretched a hand, wordlessly asking her to proceed him through the crowd. He fell back, trying to work out what it was that sparked his interest.

"This way?" she asked over her shoulder.

"Yeah." He jerked his head toward the room farthest from the bar. The one that didn't have a crowd hovering around the door. No doubt Zoe was doing her exhibitionist thing in the other private area, putting on a show with her men. "This room will soon be revamped."

At the moment, it was filled with furniture. A heap of different comfortable surfaces to rest upon. Last he'd heard, Leo and Brute wanted to turn it into a room with a more specific agenda. Restraints maybe. Role-play. They'd even spoken of development nights where they could hire people qualified to teach courses on sex and sensuality, even BDSM.

"And what type of things do people do in here?" the woman asked.

He closed his eyes, imagining it was Cassie beside him, her voice so familiar. "Whatever the hell they want, sweetheart. As long as it's consensual."

She stepped closer, the heat from her body thrumming from her in waves. "And what have you done in here?" she cooed.

Not a damn thing. "I watch," he grated. "That's it." He opened his eyes and caught sight of her lips pursed in a conniving smile.

"Would you like to watch *me*?" she whispered.

Fuck. His nostrils flared and a burst of adrenaline shot down his spine. She was a temptation, but more for the need to quash his preoccupation with Cassie than a sexual desire. He wouldn't enjoy her show, no matter what she did. Although his cock did stir at the image. The first sign of interest his dick had given the world in months.

"Not tonight." He eased a hand through her hair, trying to soften the rejection. The coarse texture ran over his palm, nothing like the silky blonde strands he'd spent years filtering his fingers through.

He turned to walk away and then froze when she grabbed his hand. He stiffened, his spine rigid as she came up behind him, hovering at his shoulder. Gentle hands encased his waist, the pleasant slide of her fingertips moved over his stomach, the softness of a womanly body melted against his back. Over the scent of sex and foreplay in the air, he could smell her, not this stranger, but his wife.

She was here. In his head. Under his skin.

"Don't be so quick to walk away." The woman sounded more like Cassie with every heartbeat. "What harm can come from watching?"

CHAPTER SEVEN

*C*assie wasn't prone to crazy outbursts. At least she hadn't been. Until now, apparently. She didn't even know what the innuendo in her own words meant. There was no plan. No strategy. Just an invitation to put on a show she didn't have the faintest clue how to perform. The only thing she knew was that she couldn't let him go. His back against her chest was too comforting, and watching him walk away again wasn't an option.

At first, she'd sat next to him at the bar, hoping to witness the level of his suffering. His emotional struggle had been clear to see. But it wasn't enough. She yearned for something else. Something she had no clue of. That's when she'd asked for a tour.

A part of her wanted to be rejected. She already knew her way around. The request was a test. An indicator. She'd held her breath, waiting for him to shoo her away, to show no interest in the appeal of a woman that he didn't know was his wife.

Then he'd caved, too easily, and a part of her heart had shattered. At the same time, the pounding in her chest had intensified, yearning for more of the ferocity in his eyes. She'd became seduced by his proximity. After the months apart, she would kill to have his hands on her. To feel his passion and adoration.

He was hooked.

To her.

He turned in her embrace, his jaw set in a stubborn line. "Let me go."

No. Not now, not ever. She did loosen her grip, though. "Don't newbies get special treatment?" Still, she had no clue where her words were coming from. This wasn't her.

She dug her teeth into her lower lip and batted her fake lashes. "You don't have to touch. You don't even have to speak. Just watch. Your eyes will tell me everything I need to know."

His discomfort gave her confidence. Too much. Because now she was backtracking to the empty single bed, hiding the grief of losing his body heat as she scooted onto the mattress. A feast, not only for his eyes, but for the numerous other patrons in the room.

He was interested in her for one reason—she was his wife. His soul mate. Nobody else here tonight could've evoked interest from him. His attraction was subconscious. She knew it was and wouldn't allow herself to believe otherwise.

She crooked a finger at him and slid farther back. This was crazy. The actions of a love-starved woman. But he was also her husband. She could do insane things for him. Anything for him.

She nestled onto the cushions, parting her thighs while she licked her lower lip in a coy taunt. Her stomach was filled with butterflies. Her heart was pounding in her throat. And despite the nerves, her nipples hardened to painful peaks and the sweet spot between her thighs began to tingle.

T.J. lifted his chin and clenched his hands at his sides

once...twice. The internal struggle was etched across his tight features. He was fighting the attraction, denying he wanted another woman. When all along it was his wife he still desired.

Slowly, she raised a hand, trailing it over the material of her slip, along her sternum, her neck, to her lips. T.J. watched the progression, his focus riveted, his hands still clenched. She sucked the finger into her mouth, all the way to the knuckle, and then released it with a pop.

She'd never been so blatant. That had always been his job. He'd taught her everything she knew about sex. His desires had shaped her own. She'd been the young, inexperienced woman about to reach her twenties when T.J. had strode into her life and ruined her for all other men.

He'd taken his time, getting to know her leisurely. Intimately. More thoroughly than she'd known herself. The sex between them had gone from casual to exploratory. By the time they'd married, she'd been willing and eager to try anything and everything.

In the past, the awe in his eyes had given her the confidence to find herself sexually. Right now, that same look gave her the ability to be on a foreign bed, observed by strangers as her finger lowered to the hem of her tiny dress and underneath to the waistband of her panties. She couldn't tear her gaze away from him. Like a hawk, she scrutinized his expression, gaining evidence of his arousal from the flaring of his nostrils and the rapid rise and fall of his chest.

"Do you want a taste?" It was a bittersweet question. Dismissal would bathe her in rejection. Acquiescence would mean he was ready to move on from their marriage. So she was thankful he didn't answer.

Still unsure what she was doing, or why, she continued the charade. She slid her hand under the lace of her underwear, the tingles of awareness igniting all over the newly skimmed flesh. She grazed the rough patch of curls at the apex of her thighs and held her breath as she drowned in the darkness of his eyes. She was on display, alone, confused, yet her body was burning with the need to be sated.

By him. Only him.

Her husband inched forward, his large frame a menacing force at the end of the bed. He was riveted with her, his jaw tight, his hands still clenched, yet those deep irises were enthralled with her alluring display. Hypnotized.

She crept her hand lower, closing her eyes briefly when her fingertips found her clit. The tiny bundle of nerves was throbbing. Begging. Pleading with every rush of blood and pound of her heart to be sated beyond her wildest imagination. Here. In front of all these people.

Pleasure took over, her fingers moved of their own accord as they rubbed back and forth, tearing a gasp from her throat.

"You should stop." His words barely penetrated the pounding heartbeat echoing in her ears. "I need to get back to work."

She quirked a brow when he didn't leave. Rejection would soon be upon her. It was inevitable. But her mask would hide the humiliation. It was already shielding her from the intensity of numerous people who had stopped their own play sessions to see if she would succeed in seducing this glorious man.

With a dramatic sigh, she slid her hand from her panties and crawled toward him. He backtracked, cautiously leaving space between them as if she were a predator ready to pounce. The contrasting dynamic was unnerving. T.J. had always been the dominant force. He never backed away. He always inspired the need to please him. The desire to succumb. She thrived on the way her heart, mind and body submitted wholeheartedly to his instructions. Now she was in the lead and wasn't sure what to do with the power.

She stood, allowing a few brief seconds for her jelly legs to strengthen before she sauntered toward him on her heels. Her gaze held his as she approached. The room fell silent, and the pressure of anticipation pressed hard against her skin. There was a breath of space between them when she planted her feet and peered up at him with a coy smile.

"Touch me." Her heart hammered behind her ribs. It was becoming harder to disguise her voice. Everything inside her urged her to stop pretending. To quit hiding.

"I can't." His fierce tone was almost inaudible. "I've gotta go." Again, he didn't move. He held his chin high. His shoulders were broad and eyes intense as he frowned. "I just don't understand."

"Understand what, T.J.?" She raised a hand, her touch almost reaching his cheek when he lifted his arm in a flash and a heavy force gripped her wrist.

"Understand your familiarity," he growled. His gaze narrowed, the softness she'd always seen in the brown depths now harsh and unforgiving. "How do you know my name?"

Oh, heck. Her lips worked as she struggled to figure out her answer, his grip unyielding. "You work here." She managed a fake grin. "The man at the door told me your name."

He jerked back, his eyes clouding with confusion as he released his hold. "I'm...sorry."

"Don't be." She bridged the distance between them again and rested her palms on his hard chest. She missed this expanse of skin. The hard muscle that used to keep her protected at night. "Sometimes attraction can be confusing." She glided her hands higher, over his shoulders, around his neck. "Sometimes it can be clarifying, too, like the world is sending you a sign."

She was going to tell him. As soon as her heart stopped pounding, she was going to remove her wig and prove he would always be attracted to her. "You want me," she whispered.

He sucked in a breath, the rampant beat of his chest echoing into hers as she leaned into him.

"You want me just as bad as I want you." Her stomach was overcome with excitement. With passion. In her mind, she wasn't wearing a mask, or a wig, or fake nails. She was the normal Cassie, whispering words of endearment to a husband who had lost faith. It was just the two of them. No sex club. No witnesses.

She pushed up on the tips of her toes and pressed her mouth against his, kissing love back between them. He stiffened, dropping his hands to her hips. She wasn't sure if he was poised to pull her closer or ready to push her away, but she didn't care. She gripped him tighter as she parted his lips with her tongue, unable to deny herself even a second of his confused acquiescence.

Don't let me go.

She clung to him, kissing him harder, pressing her breasts into him as she reveled in the only physical affection he'd given her in over twelve months. This was her home—in his arms. This was her life—striving for more of his love.

She stepped closer, moving one thigh between his, brushing her pelvis against the thickness of his erection. The comforting feel of his arousal rekindled hope. Their bodies were meant to be like this. Brushing. Touching. Always connected. She tilted her pelvis, rubbing her pubic bone against the hardness of his leg. Her pussy was begging for him. Soaking her panties. Every inch of her wanted to be consumed. She was merely waiting for him to take over. For her husband to find his usual dominance and use it against her.

Her excitement grew, the pleasure inside her morphing into a need more necessary than breath. She loved this man.

So much it hurt and healed, all at once. But it was his hands, the relaxation of his grip against her hips, his surrender to the affection, that washed away the desire and filled her with nauseating clarity.

She was kissing her husband. Reuniting passion. Yet *he* was kissing a stranger. Extinguishing the memory of their marriage and moving on.

The truth filled her with agony. Their connection becoming bittersweet.

With every brush of his tongue, he was leaving her. And she'd been the one to help him take the first step.

CHAPTER EIGHT

T.J. closed his eyes at the taste of her lips. It was like coming home, her mouth achingly familiar and yet punishingly different. This woman kissed like Cassie, with slow sweeps of her tongue and tiny whimpers of yearning.

He sank into the well-known sensation. Devouring it. Savoring her taste, her essence. Even breathing deep of the perfume he remembered she loved so much. It was his wife. He was kissing Cassie. At least that's what he imagined he was doing.

His tongue tangled with hers, unable to get enough. No longer willing to hold back. He gave her everything he had. He showed his devotion with the trail of his hands over her back. He displayed his attraction by the grinding of his erection against her abdomen.

He was delirious with the need to have her again. Just one more night. One more kiss before the divorce was final.

"T.J.," she whispered into his mouth.

"Cassie."

She stiffened at the name. *Hell*. This wasn't his wife—his

love. This was no one. A stranger. Some stray woman who'd dissolved his commitment to his marriage with barely a blink of her fake lashes. He stumbled back, his lips burning, his chest hollow.

What the fuck had happened?

One minute he'd been at the bar drowning his sorrows, the next he was betraying everything he held dear. It didn't make sense. This woman, although not his type, could have any man. Yet she'd come to him.

"Why did they tell you my name?" His voice was accusatory. "Why would anyone tell you who I was?"

Leo had admitted earlier they weren't sure he was going to show up tonight. They thought he was fragile. Incapable of working. So why would they point him out to new members? Why would they try penetrating his grief bubble unless they were attempting to burst it?

She stepped into him, her palm landing on his clothed chest, scorching the skin underneath. "You intrigued me. From the moment I walked in, I wanted to get to know you."

Liar. He'd acted like a drunken bum all night—sitting at the bar, sulking into a glass of scotch. Unless she was a glutton for rejection, she was hiding something. And he was certain he knew what it was.

They'd set him up—Leo, Brute, Shay. There was no other reason for her to know who he was. His business partners—his *friends*—had gone against his wishes and calculated a plan to get his mind off the divorce and his body craving the addictive release of sex.

They had no right to do this to him. He hadn't consciously made the choice to find another lover. Moving on had turned into a mess of indecision that had been taken out of his hands. The last thing he wanted was to hurt Cassie. But he just had. Even if she never found out.

He grazed a rough hand over his lips, wiping away the woman's taste. The guilt of betrayal weighed on his shoulders as anger built in his chest. Tonight was a mistake. He couldn't move on. At least not now. Not until the divorce was final. Maybe longer—weeks, months. Hell, if he didn't kiss another woman in the years to come, it'd be too soon.

"You don't think I know what you're up to?" he seethed. Somewhere, deep down, he knew it wasn't her fault. He'd succumbed on his own. Had become too entangled in delusions and the need for comfort that he'd strayed. "I know exactly why you're here. And let me tell you, honey, it ain't gonna work. You need to leave."

This wasn't Cassie. She was nothing like the woman he loved with her cheap nails and tawdry red lips. *Jesus.* He rubbed the back of his neck and struggled for calm. He wanted to vomit. To fall to his knees and never get up. At least not until the bitterness washed away.

The woman's cheeks paled, her eyes widening in horror. "But...T.J."

There she went with his name again.

"You don't think I worked it out?" His voice grew louder, the anger seeping through his words. "That I don't know who you are?" He still wasn't sure if she was a paid escort or an interested clubber with the desire for a challenge, but she was playing him nonetheless. That was enough for him. "Leave before I get security to kick you out."

She stepped away from him, as if finally realizing she'd been caught in her little game of lies. "But...I..." Her focus flew to the door, to the crowd of people gathering.

"Tanya?" Zoe pushed through the bodies crowding the entrance to the room, followed close behind by Shay. "What's going on?"

Tanya. He'd never forget that name, or the rage it solicited. "Get her out of here." Their hovering presence only cemented the betrayal. He wouldn't be surprised if they'd been watching, waiting for the deed to be done.

He shot the woman a glare, letting his disgust become evident before turning to Shay. "I don't want to see her down here again." The crowd parted as he stormed forward, coming face-to-face with Brute.

"You causing trouble?" His friend's voice was a threat.

T.J. shouldered past him, seething as he headed for the bathroom. He was in mourning. Senseless from stupidity. If he didn't find space to be alone, he'd lose himself.

His footsteps echoed in his ears as he bypassed the small crowd of underwear-clad patrons and made his way into the next private room. Zoe's companions were on the bed, both their faces filled with concern as T.J. continued forward, shoving past the bathroom door and into the calm, cool silence.

He had a few seconds, barely even time to take a deep breath or utter a greeting to the two men at the sink, before Brute stormed into the small space, followed by Leo.

"*Out.*" Brute jerked a thumb over his shoulder, not sparing their paying customers any pleasantries in his request for privacy. "If you stand watch at the door, I'll comp your next entrance fee."

The men nodded, wordlessly leaving the room, the door swinging shut behind them.

The bathroom became quiet, allowing the pounding in T.J.'s head to grow louder. Deafening. His business was meant to be where his future lay. It was meant to be the distraction from the agony. The solace from the guilt.

"Care to explain?" Leo crossed his arms over his chest.

T.J. gave a derisive laugh and strode for the basin counter. He clutched the cold marble in his hands, letting his head fall. Breath after breath soaked his lungs, as he tried to wipe the memory of the kiss from his mind and the burn still marring his lips.

"You'd want to start talking." Brute's tone was lethal. "You fucked up in front of paying clients. You better have a good reason."

T.J. closed his eyes. Was this the end? Not only of his marriage, but his friendship with Leo and Brute? They'd crossed the line. He wasn't sure if he could come back from that. There was no trust. No understanding. *Fuck.* He was losing his mind.

"I was already getting sick to death of your moping," Brute continued. "But I won't stand for outbursts in the club. And I sure as hell won't allow you to upset patrons."

T.J.'s vision darkened and his knuckles pulsed to the point of pain, his grip tightening against the counter. "I don't care how sick of my moping you are—" he swung around, his chest heaving, "—you don't pay a fucking hooker in the hopes I'll miraculously get over my wife."

Brute didn't retreat, didn't show any sign of concern. The only reaction he gave was the contortion of his features that transformed into a look of incredulity. "What the hell are you talking about?"

T.J. clenched his jaw and spoke through gritted teeth. "Don't patronize me. Did you really think I wouldn't work it out? That I was that stupid?"

Brute gave Leo a questioning look. "Do you know what he's rambling about?"

Leo shook his head. "I'm lost."

"That woman," T.J. sneered. "The one you paid to seduce me. You'll be happy to know she did her job. Although, maybe not to the extent you wanted."

"Paid?" Leo ran a hand through his loose hair. "Why would we pay someone to fuck you when half the women down here would happily do it for free?"

Semantics. "The woman you propositioned then." The perplexed way they blinked back at him drove his anger to new heights. He didn't expect Brute to understand how momentous their betrayal was. The guy had a heart for one reason, and it had nothing to do with emotion and everything to do with blood flow. But Leo was different. He understood love and the inability to control it.

"I'm still clueless." Leo shrugged.

T.J. closed his eyes and leaned back against the counter, trying to stop the room from spinning. This didn't add up. Brute was a heartless asshole. Most importantly, he was an *honest* heartless asshole. He wouldn't continue with a charade this long.

"There was a woman," he grated. "She wanted to sleep with me."

Brute's laugh was harsh. Humorless. "Man, you're so far outta the game you have no clue."

T.J. opened his eyes, glaring. "What does that mean?"

"A woman wanted to fuck you and you blame me?" Brute scoffed. "Jesus. Do you think I give a shit about your sex life?"

"So, you deny having anything to do with it?" He straightened and pinned Brute and then Leo with a stare. "It must've been Shay. Your girlfriend is poking her nose where it doesn't belong."

"No, she isn't." Leo squared his shoulders and stepped forward. "Apart from holding an unfavorable amount of concern for you, she hasn't done anything wrong."

"Even if one of us did, what's the big deal?" Brute stepped forward, scowling. "You're single."

Single in title only. His heart was still taken. His soul, too.

"Forget it." He was stupid to think they'd understand. Neither of them had a clue what it was like to love unequivocally. Undeniably. They were virgins when it came to devotion.

"No." Brute loomed closer, his emotionless façade faltering under the anger in his eyes. "You've caused a shit fight out there and I want to know why."

"Get outta my face." T.J. shoved Brute's chest, unwilling to be the stand-up guy this time. They'd pushed his kindness too far. He was entitled to his own slice of brutality.

Brute's eyes widened with the assault, then in a blink, the shock disappeared, replaced with fury. He lunged forward, swinging T.J. around until his back was up against the wall with a tight hand around his throat. "Answer me."

T.J. smirked, itching for a fight. They'd never expect it from him. He was the level-headed neutral party. He broke up brawls and dissolved arguments. He was the damn A-class citizen who made up for his dirty proclivities by being a stand-up guy, every single day of his goddamn life.

Not tonight.

"*Brute*," Leo warned.

"Answer me."

The hand around T.J.'s neck tightened and he enjoyed the panic that cleared his mind of heartache. "Go to hell."

Brute gave a feral smile. "I've been there for years, my friend. It's nice for you to finally come for a visit."

The tight grip loosened, allowing T.J. to rest his head against the cool tile. Life was never meant to be this hard. He'd been kind to everyone—his friends, his staff, his family. He was the gentleman. The comforter. He didn't deserve this. He was sacrificing his marriage for Cassie's happiness after all. This was for her future.

"I still fucking love her, okay?" He didn't move. Didn't open his eyes. He couldn't. "I don't want to live without her. I never did. But it's the only option. For her sake, I have to give her up."

"Why?" Brute's tone was murderous as his hand fell away.

"It's a long story."

"We've got time," Brute grated through clenched teeth.

T.J. released the air tightening his lungs, hoping it would lessen the pain in his chest. "Because love isn't a good enough reason to destroy someone." He opened his eyes and wished the two men staring back at him with curiosity could understand. "And that's exactly what will happen if we stay together."

CHAPTER NINE

Cassie was trembling—her arms, her legs, her chest. She couldn't breathe. Everyone was staring at her, their pity shrouding her like a dirty blanket as T.J. stormed from the room.

She hung her head and covered her face with her hands, fighting back the need to cry.

"Come with me."

A feminine hand came to rest on Cassie's back and she raised her gaze to find Shay standing beside her.

"It's going to be okay." Zoe approached. "We'll sort this out."

No. She shook her head. It wouldn't be okay. It wouldn't get sorted out. T.J. had made it perfectly clear he no longer wanted her. He'd seen through her disguise, humiliated her and demanded she leave.

"Trust me." Shay placed pressure on Cassie's back, guiding her forward. "Let's go upstairs where it's quiet."

All Cassie wanted to do was go home. But her house was filled with loneliness and despair. There was nobody there to comfort her. With a silent nod, she allowed them to lead her into the main room, bypassing the curious stares of patrons and straight past the secured door. The change rooms were a blur. The staircase upstairs was taken with no memory at all. They reached the deserted Shot of Sin bar and wordlessly guided her onto a stool.

"Do you want to talk about it?" Zoe asked, rubbing her warm palm in circles over the nakedness of Cassie's upper back.

"Come on, honey." Shay slid a glass of water over the bar, the swatch of lace over her eyes still perfectly in place. "You can tell us."

The burn of humiliation heated Cassie's cheeks. These were the last people she should tell. The thought of even explaining to Jan when she got home stung more than she could bear.

"I know I don't look suitably dressed," Shay continued. "But I've worked here for a while. I'm sure whatever happened with T.J. was a misunderstanding. Usually, he's a really nice guy. He's just going through a rough patch at the moment."

Rough patch? It was demeaning that the destruction of Cassie's marriage could be described in such simple terms. "I know." She met the sympathy in the bartender's expression. "I also know who you are, Shay."

The woman frowned and ceased pouring the glass of wine she'd been preparing. "I'm sorry," she spoke with a cautionary tone and slipped the strip of lace covering her eyes to her forehead, scrutinizing Cassie, "but I can't place your face under the disguise."

"We've never actually met." Cassie grasped the bottom of her mask and sighed as she lifted the covering from her face. She shouldn't be doing this. These were T.J.'s friends. *His* support network. Not hers.

"I've heard a lot about you through my husband." She

raised the mask over her head and met the bartenders gaze. "I'm T.J.'s wife, Cassie."

Shay's eyes widened, but it was Zoe's gasp that made Cassie swivel on her stool. "I'm sorry I lied about my name. I didn't want to risk being thrown out."

Zoe shook her head, her lips gaping. "I'm not offended. I'm shocked T.J.'s married. He's never made it known to guests. I always assumed he was single."

He hadn't made his marriage known. In a sex club, surrounded by women and men grasping for carnality and pleasure, he hadn't told the members he was taken. Nobody knew of their love. Why did that knowledge fill her with horror?

"Don't panic." Zoe reached out a hand and squeezed Cassie's shoulder. "I've never seen him with anyone. I rarely see him downstairs at all. It was merely an assumption."

Cassie played with the elastic band on her mask, occupying her hands because she had no control over her mind.

"I didn't know until recently either," Shay added. "I think he's far too much of a gentleman to share his personal details in a work environment."

Yes, maybe that was it. He'd admitted long ago that he didn't want her being a part of the sex club. Not until they had measures in place to safeguard the identity of everyone involved.

"He's protective." Cassie lowered her gaze to her lap, threading the elastic through her fingers. "I used to attend work functions years ago. But once they started chatting about opening Vault of Sin, T.J. wanted me as far away from the business as possible. He didn't want to risk my involvement if the privacy of the club was ever breeched."

"Hold up." Shay leaned forward, into Cassie's periphery.

"If he's so protective, why did he let you in tonight? What was the fight about?"

Cassie met the woman's gaze with a wince. "He didn't let me in. I used a fake ID."

"Oh, shit. Brute is gonna be pissed that you slipped past him."

"Not as pissed as T.J. was when he found out he was kissing his wife instead of a stranger."

Shay's mouth gaped. "He didn't know?"

Cassie shook her head and grabbed the front of her hairpiece. "I went to a lot of effort to make myself unrecognizable." She pulled the wig off her head and placed it on the bar. "I'm blonde." She mussed her hair, trying to form some semblance of normality from the plastered-down strands she could see in the mirror behind the bar. "Everything about me is different. Apart from the weight. Although, I have dropped a dress size since my husband informed me of the divorce."

"Was this retaliation?" Zoe asked, sliding onto a stool.

"God, no."

"Then what?" Zoe's tone was gentle, the soft lilt filled with comfort and concern. "Why turn up at his sex club and pretend you're someone else?"

"Because I love him." Cassie hung her head. "I don't want a divorce, and with every part of me, I know T.J. doesn't either."

"Then why would he request it?"

"It's complicated." She gave a derisive laugh. "Yet simplistic, too. We both made a mistake that he takes full credit for. He thinks he let me down. He's too defensive when it comes to my wellbeing."

"Okay." Shay cleared her throat. "You're going to have to go into more depth than that. I need deets."

Tension built in Cassie's chest, the need to bare her soul

itched to break free. Nobody in her day-to-day life would understand. These women were the closest she would get to a knowledgeable sounding board, and she needed to rid herself of the guilt from the past. "My marriage with T.J. was nothing but flawless—"

"Really?" Shay drawled in disbelief.

"Let me finish. We rarely fought. We meshed perfectly. He gave me everything I needed from a lover and a friend, and I tried to give him the same in return." The women were staring at her, clinging to her every word. "I learned a lot about myself because of him. Sexually speaking, I mean."

She cleared the discomfort from her throat. "As a new couple, we tried everything and anything. As time went on, we began pushing boundaries. I had limited experience when we first met, and T.J. opened my eyes to the possibilities. He made me feel comfortable fantasizing about things that aren't society's standard of normal."

"Like?"

Cassie shrugged. "It started off simple, with sex toys and classy porn."

"Classy porn?" Zoe raised a brow, a smile brightening her features. "Is that even a thing?"

"Well, there's dirty porn and there's the stuff with the faintest hint of a romantic storyline. Neither have good acting."

Zoe chuckled. "Okay. Carry on."

"That evolved into light BDSM, but apart from T.J.'s usual dominance, it wasn't our scene. We started talking about other topics like voyeurism and exhibitionism. It was around the same time the Vault was being discussed as a possible form of revenue for the business." Cassie waved the conversation away. "I'm rambling. You guys don't want to hear all this."

"Of course we do." Shay grabbed a bottle of wine from

the fridge underneath the far side of the bar. "I'll even provide refreshments."

The verbal purge didn't seem to be lessening the tight hold on Cassie's heart. It wasn't helping. Yet neither would going home to a lonely house. "To cut a long story relatively short, the reason T.J. is leaving me is because we decided to go to our first sex club about a year ago. It was out of the blue. Unplanned. In fact, we were out of town, staying in Brute's Tampa apartment. In Florida, people are open to much more than they are here. So, we went to a club on a whim... The worst whim of my life."

"You didn't like it?" Shay paused in the middle of pouring the first of three wine glasses on the bar.

"I don't think the first time is ever easy," Zoe added. "Even more so when you're in an established relationship and have to consider the possibility of how it could affect your future together."

"It was a disaster." Cassie sucked in a breath, held it until the pain took over the nerves in her belly, then released it in a rush. "It was the biggest mistake of my life."

Shay cringed. "It's not for everyone. Hell, even I was disgusted to begin with."

"That wasn't the half of it." She wrung her hands together in her lap, wiping the sweat from her palms. "For starters, I'd glamorized the thought of a sex club. I anticipated seduction and passion. Fine furnishings and men who cherished their women like T.J. cherished me. The place we went to was cold, dank and sleazy."

"That's not good." Shay slid a glass of wine toward Cassie and another in front of Zoe.

"T.J. wanted to leave straightaway. I could sense his annoyance. But the surprising conditions didn't curb my curiosity. We were out of town, finally in a place where I wouldn't feel nervous about my friends and family finding out about our sexual tendencies." Cassie placed the mask on the bar beside the wig and grabbed for the wine glass. "We'd been talking about going to a club for so long...work had already started on the Vault. And even though the scene was far from erotic, I wanted to understand what a sex club was all about. There had to be a reason why women were there, right? So, I begged T.J. to hang around, just for one drink."

She sipped her wine, the sweet taste exploding over her tongue in complete contrast to the liquid she remembered consuming that night in Tampa. The bartender—dressed in a frayed wife-beater and ill-fitting silk boxers—had leered at her as he handed over the soda glass filled with cheap wine. He was just one of many men who'd eyed her like a dish they were determined to taste.

"T.J. didn't drink. He stayed at my side, his hand always protectively placed on my hip as we watched men rut like dogs in heat. There was no seduction. No interest in pleasuring anyone but themselves. The women were merely a vessel to be used."

"Drugged?" Shay asked.

Zoe swiveled in the stool, her knee grazing Cassie's thigh. "Paid escorts, I'd assume."

"Yeah." Cassie gave Zoe a nod. "Apparently, it's not uncommon. T.J. had murmured in my ear that some clubs who can't obtain willing female clientele actually pay escorts to attend. So, in retrospect, I was like the rainbow unicorn—the one willing female who had turned up to this sleazy place without monetary compensation." She shrugged off the stupidity, because she hadn't even broached the worst part. "I made a vain attempt to salvage the night. I ignored our surroundings and tried my hardest to feel sexy as I stripped to my underwear. But my halfhearted attempt to get T.J. in the mood didn't work."

The humiliation of going down on a husband that couldn't

get hard was just as potent as how naïve she'd felt walking into an environment she had no right being in. "After twenty minutes inside that place, I'd lost all hope of exploring this part of our sexuality."

"Oh, sweetie." Zoe placed a hand on Cassie's shoulder. "You can't judge the lifestyle by one seedy club."

Cassie ran her finger mindlessly through the ring of condensation left on the bar from her glass. Time hadn't dimmed the memory of that night. It was the first regretful moment of her married life. One that had sparked a continuous tally of devastation.

"It gets worse," she uttered. "Our apartment was a half-hour drive away, so I decided to use the bathroom before we left. T.J. did the same. It was the first time he'd strayed from my side, and he wasn't happy about it either. He told me he'd be waiting right outside the bathroom door once he finished, and that I shouldn't speak to anyone while we were separated."

She stared at the polished bar, seeing the memory replay in her mind. T.J. had been pale with concern, extinguishing the adrenaline in her veins and replacing it with fear. He'd clutched her biceps, reiterating that she wasn't to speak to anyone. Not even the women.

She'd nodded, and done as he requested, entering the empty bathroom and using the facilities as quickly as possible. She'd been poised to flush the toilet when the swing of the bathroom door had announced someone else had entered. As she'd clutched her handbag to her waist, she'd opened the stall door, prepared to keep her head low while she washed her hands and then get straight back to T.J.'s side.

"A man followed me into the bathroom." He'd been one of the younger men, somewhere in his late twenties, she guessed. Tall and scrawny with the glaze of a drug-fueled high in his eyes. "At first, I thought maybe he was disoriented.

That he'd picked the wrong bathroom. But he showed no shock at seeing me walk from the stall. He'd known I was in there."

The recollection was vivid. He'd had oily blond hair and a sharp, bird-like nose. His eyes had been devoid of emotion, light blue and feral. There'd been no defining scars, only a permanent frown on his forehead. But his boxer briefs were what she remembered most. Probably because the image of his erection pressing against the crotch still made nausea creep up her throat.

"I smiled, somewhat nervously, as I approached the basin to wash my hands. I joked about him being in the wrong bathroom. Although something inside me was screaming to run, I didn't want to act like a fool in case he'd made a genuine mistake." Her ears filled with silence, her mind consumed with memories. "He made no move to leave. Instead, he approached me. And again, I did nothing. I kept denying what was clearly happening. I didn't think that a man would ever try to hurt me in a public place with my husband in the bathroom next door."

It had been too blatant to be real. Nobody could be that stupid. But apparently, she had been. "He started talking, his words slurred as he asked what my plans were for the night. He wanted to know why I was there. If I was unsatisfied with my current lover since it was obvious T.J. wasn't in the mood."

She'd washed her hands, tracking him in the mirror as he continued to approach. "He'd been watching us. *Me*. And my pathetic attempts to try and go down on T.J." It made her feel dirty, but there still hadn't been any confirmed threat, nothing apart from intuition screaming at her to leave. "I assured him I was there out of curiosity, and that I'd decided this was no longer a lifestyle choice I was interested in. I began to walk for the door when he stepped in front of me, blocking my path."

He'd seemed to ponder her words as his gaze raked her body in a way she'd never experienced before. He was sizing her up, determining something she couldn't or didn't want to understand. "I didn't want to scream. I had already started blaming myself. If I hadn't gone there, this man wouldn't have had the wrong impression of me. He thought I was an easy lay, and I wasn't. I tried to talk him down, assuring him I wouldn't be going back into the main room."

His eyes had been vacant, icy-blue irises that reflected an empty soul. The first step he'd taken toward her had made her realize she needed to act. It finally sank in. He was a threat and she needed to get out of there. "I'm not interested." She'd raised her chin and glared at him as her head had begun to pound with too many thoughts to comprehend what to do. Did she try to hurt him? Did she run? Was T.J. right outside the door like he'd promised, or had something happened to him too? "I'll scream."

"Hey." Zoe's hand came to rest on Cassie's back again, rubbing in soothing circles. "You're safe now."

Cassie tried to shake away the nightmare, but he kept approaching. "It didn't go much further." She didn't want to relive the way his hand had lashed out, climbing under her loose skirt to tear away her G-string before she could scream. "I called for help, and T.J. was there in an instant. My husband was unrecognizable, his expression contorted in anguish and rage as he threw the guy to the floor and started pounding his fists into the man's face. Again and again and again. More people entered the room as the bastard on the floor stopped fighting back."

Cassie met the distraught features of each woman in turn, both of them riveted by her story. "They had to drag T.J. off him." He'd been rabid. Crazed. "He was yelling as they hauled him from the building. His voice was so loud, demanding they let go, shouting for them to get their hands off me as they yanked me along after him. Their greedy palms touching me in places I wish I could forget."

She didn't remember how they arrived back at the apartment, and the memories after that were like photographs. Snapshots. She'd sat on the shower floor, hugging her knees to her chest as the water cascaded over her body. The darkness of the room as she lay in bed, while the sound of T.J. vomiting carried from the bathroom. The muted plane ride home. And the silence they'd both shared for the weeks that followed.

"He wanted to call the police. That night, he even drove to a nearby police station. But I couldn't do it." She squeezed her eyes shut briefly. "There were too many reasons to keep my mouth shut. I'd placed myself in that position. I'd been stupid. I know it doesn't excuse what happened. I just couldn't risk public scrutiny either. My family would've been devastated. I would've lost my job or been pressured to quit from the nastiness of others. But the determining factor was Vault of Sin. T.J., Leo and Brute are loyal men. I didn't want them to contemplate abandoning their plans for the private part of the club to spare my dignity. So, I told T.J. I didn't want anyone knowing. Not the police, not family and definitely not our business partners."

They'd never discussed what happened with anyone. T.J. had barely mentioned the night in the last twelve months. Yet, she refused to feel guilty about opening her mouth now. If it meant saving her marriage, she'd disclose every last detail, her pride and reputation be damned.

"That asshole deserves to be shot," Shay seethed.

Cassie inclined her head. "Yeah. It wasn't the best experience I've ever had. Then again, I was lucky T.J. saved me. It just wasn't enough for him. He blames himself, and I think what happened destroyed him more than me. I never truly got him back after that night."

He hadn't been able to look at her for weeks. He couldn't touch her without his eyes glazing as he lost himself to hindsight. In his mind, the blame over not researching the club rested solely on his shoulders, with him unwilling to let her take any responsibility. He considered it his own weakness for succumbing to the temptation of exposing her to something new. He thrived on broadening her sex life and wouldn't forgive himself for rushing in unprepared.

"A month passed before he started sleeping on the couch, claiming he didn't want to keep me awake with his restlessness. That night turned into every night until I started noticing the spare bed was being slept in. Six months later, he moved out."

"I need to clear my head. Just a few days. Maybe a week."

He'd been exceptionally agitated the day he'd walked from their home. As if the months of guilt had collided, and she'd had no desire to hurt him more by making him stay.

"I don't know what to say," Shay whispered.

Cassie met her gaze and winced at the sorrow shining back at her. "There's nothing *to* say. I didn't want to believe he was serious about the divorce, but after tonight, I think it's clear he can't get over the past. He's never looked at me in anger before."

She sipped her wine, uncomfortable in the silence with these women who were practically strangers. The chatter of people in the distance was all she could hear until footsteps echoed up the Vault staircase, the pounding getting louder.

"Quick," Shay blurted. "Put the wig back on. The mask, too."

Cassie's heart throttled to high speed. Although T.J. knew she was here, she didn't want anyone else to find out.

As Shay straightened and Zoe turned to face the stairway, Cassie hitched the fake hair back into position and slid the mask into place. She was still straightening the stray strands of hair sticking out at odd angles when the footsteps stopped.

"Ladies." Leo's honeyed tone filled her belly with nerves. "There seems to be a misunderstanding that I need to get to the bottom of." The pounding of his shoes against the floor sounded again, getting closer and closer. "T.J. is under the impression someone paid an escort to seduce him."

What? Cassie's gaze snapped to Shay, hoping to gain some understanding while she kept her back to her business partner.

"I thought you said he knew you were here," Zoe muttered under her breath.

He did. T.J. had whispered her name as they'd kissed. Right before he'd demanded she leave.

"Shay." The name was a deeply masculine growl. "Please tell me you don't know anything about this. I assured T.J. my adorably sweet girlfriend wouldn't be stupid enough to risk her job by getting involved."

Shay released a nervous chuckle. "Honey, you say the nicest things, but your tone implies you don't think I'm that sweet."

"Yeah," he grated. "I should work on that."

Shay strode around the bar and sauntered toward Leo. Cassie swiveled in her stool, keeping her face shadowed by her hair as Shay stopped in front of her boyfriend and leaned to whisper something in his ear.

As the faint hint of her words drifted forward, Leo's scrutinizing gaze snapped to Cassie. His frown deepened, the wrinkles increasing with each passing second until Shay stepped back.

"What's going on here?" Leo approached, shoving his hands in his pockets in a vain attempt to appear nonchalant.

Zoe scooted to the side of her stool, turning her knees into Cassie. "If you want to leave right now, no questions asked, just tell me. I'll escort you out. You don't need to speak to him. We can go somewhere else and talk about this."

We. Such a simple word, yet the friendship behind it brought an explosion of warmth through Cassie's body. "Thank you, but I think he deserves to know why I caused the scene downstairs."

Zoe inclined her head. "It's up to you."

Cassie removed her mask and checked her reflection in the mirror across the bar. There wouldn't be any beauty awards heading her way in the near future, and even without the mask, she was still barely recognizable.

She pushed from the stool and straightened her shoulders as she faced Leo, a man she'd met numerous times but didn't claim to know well enough to anticipate how he'd react. She gave him a sad smile and pulled off her wig, exposing the blonde hair beneath.

He squinted at her, his gaze raking her face, then lower, all the way to her high-heel-covered toes.

"Fake nails." She placed the wig on the bar and wiggled her fingers. "Fake tan." She indicated her body with a wave of her hand. "Contact lenses." She pointed to her eyes. "All of it's fake."

"Oh, shit." His voice was barely audible. "Cassie? Is that really you?"

She gave a regretful nod. "Hi, Leo."

"*Jesus Christ*." He massaged his forehead and began to pace. "I need to tell him."

"No." Cassie scooted forward, her heels tapping frantically along the floor. "Wait." She grabbed his arm as he turned to leave. "What did you mean when you said T.J. thinks someone paid an escort?"

"I mean exactly that, Cass. He's down there, almost coming to blows with Brute because he thinks the woman he was making out with was a hooker."

Cassie shook her head. "He said my name. He knew it was me."

Leo peered down at her, seeming to read her thoughts when she couldn't even understand them herself. "You can interpret it however you like, but he's down there thinking he cheated on his wife. He has no clue you're here."

"He doesn't?" She felt like a parrot, repeating the words in her head over and over again. But if he didn't know she was here, why had he said her name? "He must have been thinking about me." A smile tilted her lips. A weak, almost useless smile that filled her aching heart with hope.

Then whiplash had her straightening. He may have been *thinking* about her. However, to his knowledge, he'd been kissing someone else. He'd cheated on her...*with* her.

"Cassie, I'm sorry, I know you're hurting." Leo stroked her cheek with his knuckles. "But you have to leave. I can't be a part of this, not only because he's my business partner. He's my friend above all else."

"And he's my husband." She swallowed over the dryness in her throat and dropped her hold on his arm. "I'll do anything to get him back."

"We'll figure out another plan together," Shay offered.

"Shay," Leo warned. "I don't want to hear this."

"Then run along, sweetheart."

His ocean-blue irises darkened with contempt. "You don't understand. T.J. is going out of his mind. He's beside himself. I've never seen him so distraught."

"That can only work in Cassie's favor." The sound of Zoe's footsteps approached. "If there's still emotional attachment, surely there has to be a way to stop the divorce."

"You both need to stay out of it," Leo grated. "We won't stand for drama in the club. No matter who's involved. Tonight has been bad enough. The only saving grace for you, Cass, is that he has no clue it was you."

Drama hadn't been her intent. She hadn't even planned to seduce him. That was a bonus. One that would've kicked her in the balls if she had any. "I'm sorry for the stress I caused. I just can't let him go. I know he still loves me."

Leo inclined his head. "I know that, too."

Wait. What? "You do?"

"Yes." His tone was comforting even though a scowl creased his forehead. "You don't understand what's going on downstairs. I've just spent the last ten minutes holed up in the bathroom with him. He's spilling secrets and losing his shit. It's obvious he loves you."

This was the first true glimmer of hope. Doubt had started to whittle away the certainty of T.J.'s affection. Now her confidence was renewed. "He told you about the other club." It wasn't a question. She could see understanding in his eyes.

He nodded and gave her a somber smile. "He mentioned it. Among other things. And to be honest, I understand his reasons for the divorce. Maybe it's for the best."

The meager glimpse of hope shattered, leaving her chest hollow. It wasn't Leo's words. It was the pity in his expression. The complete lack of belief for any happiness in her future.

"How?" Shay accused. "One bad decision shouldn't end a marriage. How could he leave her after what had happened? If anything, he should be ashamed for not sticking by her. He'd walked out when she needed him the most."

Leo inclined his head. "He has a lot of regret. But this isn't about one mistake. There are ongoing issues that led to his decision."

"Ongoing issues?" Cassie reached out a hand, needing grounding, needing something. Anything. Then she let her arm fall back to her side. "Tell me. If there's more, I deserve to know."

"I'm not willing to get involved. Not any more than I already have." He held up his hands in surrender. "I won't."

Searing pain seeped into Cassie's heart. The harder she pushed for answers, the less clarity came. There couldn't be more reasons to the divorce. She refused to believe that. They'd been happy. Hadn't they? Or had she taken steps along the contented path on her own?

"Well, maybe there are things I'm no longer willing to do for you either," Shay cooed.

Leo turned to his girlfriend, hitting her with a confident stare that spoke of his disbelief. "You need to stay out of it."

Shay crossed her arms over her chest. "While I'm staying out of it, there's something you'll be staying out of, too." A feral smirk tilted her lips. "My pussy."

"Thanks for the clarification, sweetheart. I wouldn't have figured out what you meant otherwise." He rolled his eyes and turned back to Cassie with a shrug. "Look, this is your life and your marriage. I'm not going to dictate what you should do. But I need to respect T.J.'s decision." He grabbed her hand, kissed her knuckles and released his hold just as quickly. "I hope you can work it out."

He walked away, his heavy steps echoing through the club before he disappeared behind the door leading downstairs.

"So, where do we go from here?" Shay stepped into Cassie's vision, shattering her concentration.

"*We* don't go anywhere." These women were lovely. Without encouragement, they'd befriended her and helped to pick her up after the humiliation downstairs. "Thank you both for being so kind to me. I appreciate it."

It was time to leave. Her mind was filled with fog, her heart torn in two from the emotional blows too numerous to recall. She needed to get home and lick her wounds. To see if she could pick herself back up and return to the battlefield when she now had no clue who or what her enemy was.

"Don't listen to him." Shay waved a hand toward the doorway Leo had fled behind. "Whatever happens, he'll get over it."

"Shay, maybe you *should* stay out of it." Zoe came to stand beside Cassie. "I can help where possible."

"No." Cassie strode for the bar and snatched the wig off the counter. She tugged it back on and stared at her reflection in the mirror, instantly wanting to scratch the itch from her scalp. "Both of you should stay out of it. The last thing I want to do is undermine T.J."

She turned and gave them a fake smile. "I'll be fine."

Zoe approached and helped position the wig back in place. "Do you have a plan?"

Cassie shook her head. She didn't have anything. Apparently, she didn't even have the real reason why T.J. wanted a divorce. "I have determination. And for now, that's all I need."

CHAPTER TEN

*T*hree days later, Cassie was still numb as she drove home from the supermarket. She'd spent every waking moment trying to figure out what could've caused the need for a divorce if it hadn't been the assault in the sex club. There was no answer. Not even a clue. And even worse, she didn't have a plan to win T.J. back either.

At least she was eating again. Her lack of appetite had fallen prey to the need to binge, and she currently had a car full of junk food.

Soon she'd need to accept that her husband wasn't coming back. No matter how much he still loved her. His stubborn streak was going to win, and she was going to end up alone.

She turned onto her street and eased off the accelerator at the sight of an unfamiliar car parked in her driveway. She wasn't prone to fits of apprehension over foreign vehicles, but after T.J. had surprised her with the divorce, she was skeptical of any strangers that came to visit.

Her fingers skimmed the garage clicker and she pressed the button to open the door. As she passed the vehicle to her left, she glimpsed long dark hair. A woman. Great. Maybe today's surprise would be sponsored by a pregnant mistress or jealous girlfriend.

Pulling the car to a stop, she grabbed her handbag and yanked it to her side in a vain attempt for comfort. She fled the vehicle, her chin held high, her limbs heavy from exhaustion. As she pasted a smile on her lips, she came face-to-face with a gorgeous brunette at the trunk of her car.

The woman's features were shaded by the Sinner baseball cap she wore, her loose T-shirt and short shorts exposing an enviable figure.

"Shay?" Cassie squinted into the sun.

"I look different with my clothes on, don't I?" Shay smiled, resurrecting the comforting friendship from Thursday. "So do you."

"What are you doing here?"

"I'm not really here. I'm at the gym." Her smile widened. "I wanted to see how you were feeling after the other night."

Cassie winced through the painful reminder and chose to deflect. "Do you want to come inside for a coffee?"

"Love to."

Cassie ignored the bags of groceries on her backseat and ushered Shay into the house. The woman was gorgeous, her face brighter in the daylight. The gleam of mischief in her eyes sparked an unnerving sense of foreboding.

"What's the plan of attack?" Shay rubbed her hands together and rested back into the dining room chair.

"No plan." Not yet anyway, and she was running out of time. "I thought you weren't meant to get involved."

"It seems I have a problem with authority. Usually, when I'm told not to do something, it makes it impossible for me to stay away. And besides, making Leo angry is a major turn-on."

"Is he the one who told you where I live?" Having Leo on her side would be a step in the right direction. Whatever T.J.

was going through, he needed his friends, and if those friends were supporting her endeavors to win him back, it would make her life easier.

"I can't divulge how I came about that information. Let's just say I'd be in a lot of trouble if your husband or my boyfriend found out."

Cassie nodded, trying to hide her disappointment.

"So where are you going from here? I thought I might see you back at the club on Saturday night."

"No. I wasn't interested in making the same mistake twice." She'd tried and failed in her first attempt to get close to her husband. "On Friday, I went in search of legal representative to help fight the divorce. Everyone I called was enthusiastic about taking my money to gain more assets in the settlement, but that's not what I'm after. I want my husband. I want my marriage. Nobody could understand that."

Cassie stared blankly into her coffee, seeing nothing but T.J. in her vision. "The only way I can stop the proceedings is to convince him to change his mind, and I'm no longer confident I can do that."

"Hey." Shay's voice was strong. Firm. Even a little angry. "You can't give up."

Cassie lifted her gaze and was hit with the determination in Shay's fierce brown eyes. "I don't want to give up. But at some point, I'm going to have to. I know he's making a mistake, and one day he'll realize it, too. I'm just not sure how long I'm willing to fight while I wait for him to figure it out. I've lost a year of my life anticipating the return of our perfect marriage." She swallowed over the tightness in her throat. "When am I allowed to give up?"

"Not yet, that's for sure. You need to try harder."

Cassie sighed. "I don't know if I can. It hurts too much."

The worst of it came at night, when she was alone in her bed, nothing but blankets to comfort her.

"It'll hurt more once there's no hope. The divorce isn't final yet."

"No, but he kissed someone else. At least that's what he thinks. He's already moving on."

Shay leaned forward, demanding Cassie's full attention. "He's struggling. He won't talk to anyone. Whatever that kiss meant to him wasn't good, I assure you. I think he hates himself for it."

Cassie winced. She didn't want to take pleasure in his suffering, but a tiny part of her did. Something inside her burned to life with the knowledge he was as miserable as she was. "What can I do?"

A sly grin tilted Shay's lips. "You hinted the other night that you owned part of the business. That you were a partner. Is that true?"

Cassie shrugged slowly. "I'm a silent partner. T.J. and I share a third of the business. I kept my own full-time job because we weren't sure the club and restaurant were going to be successful."

"Are you legally required to remain a silent partner?"

"Not that I know of." Cassie drew out her words, uncertain where the conversation was heading. "It was never really discussed. Not between T.J. and I, anyway. I'm not sure what was said to Leo and Brute." A shiver ran down her spine as Shay's lips quirked into a conniving smile. "Why? What are you thinking?"

"T.J. is trying to shut himself off to any thoughts or memories of you. He hates being reminded of his marriage. I'm sure he's striving to get you out of his mind so he can move on."

"Awesome," Cassie drawled. The realization stung. She'd never be able to get him out of her mind. In time, she may be able to dull the hurt with a fling or two, but he would always be in her heart. He'd always be a major part of her life.

"Let me finish." Shay held up a hand. "Being part owner means you can claim your rightful place as a manager of the club. Tell him you no longer want to remain a silent partner. Demand a position within the business."

Cassie shook her head. "I can't. He's left me a substantial amount of assets in the divorce in return for my share. Soon, I'll have no right to be there at all."

"*Soon*. But not yet. The divorce isn't final. You still have a few weeks, right?"

"Yeah..." She refused to count down the days.

"You know, the economy isn't great at the moment. Unemployment is at an all-time high." Shay gave a theatrical gasp and covered a hand over her mouth. "Oh, my gosh, Cass, what would you do if you lost your job? There'd be no choice. You'd have to work with your husband, at least until you found another form of income."

"You want me to quit my job?" No way. No way in hell. She was consumed with the need to fix her marriage, but she wasn't this conniving.

Shay shrugged. "How badly do you want your husband back?"

Her phone trilled from the kitchen counter, announcing an incoming message...or maybe acknowledging a winning idea. She stood and dragged her feet toward the device to cradle it in her palm. "They'll refuse. Not only T.J., Brute and Leo, too. None of them will want me there. They'll fight to make sure I can't step foot inside their club."

"*Your* club," Shay clarified. "And leave Leo to me. I have ways of encouraging his compliance."

Cassie released a halfhearted laugh. "That still leaves two."

"Lucky for us, Brute's heartlessness runs both ways. If he

thinks it's in T.J.'s best interest to stay married, he'll support you." Shay rolled her eyes. "Not that he'll go out of his way to show it. I just need to convince him that T.J. doesn't want a divorce. What he really needs is a kick in the ass."

Shay made it sound easy, and maybe, for a woman like her, it would be. Cassie wasn't as prone to making decisions that would hurt or annoy others. It was one thing to push T.J. out of his comfort zone in an effort to win him back. It was entirely another to turn his best friends against him and work her way into their business.

"I don't know..." She unlocked her phone, needing time to think, and held her breath at the sight of T.J.'s name on her screen.

"Can I come over today?"

"What is it?"

Cassie didn't realize she was smiling until she met Shay's gaze. "It's T.J. He wants to come over."

"Why?" Shay frowned.

"I don't know. I guess to talk. Maybe he's changed his mind." That was her first thought, and the one she'd cling to. Her heart was already aflutter, her belly filling with longing.

"Ask him." Shay stood and walked forward. "Don't make assumptions. Especially when the other possibilities could hurt. You need to stay in the game. Remain strong."

Cassie didn't want to think about the potential reasons for the message. She would remain positive. She had to. "So, what do I send back?"

"Give it here." Shay grabbed the phone from Cassie's hand and began typing. "There."

"*Wait*. Don't send anything." She snatched the device back and read the message Shay had already sent. *"Why? I'm kinda busy today and I thought you'd already gotten everything off your chest."*

Jesus Christ. "He'll know that didn't come from me. I've

never spoken to him like that before." She wasn't a ballbuster like Shay.

"He needs to know you're not waiting around, spending every minute trying to work out ways to get him back. He's—"

"But I am." The last thing she wanted was for her husband to think she was moving on, giving him more of an excuse to do the same.

"What he doesn't know can only help our cause. Play hardball. If he thinks you're busy, he'll wonder who with. At least until we find out what he wants."

The phone vibrated in her hands seconds before the trill of the incoming message.

It doesn't need to be today. I only want to pick up my stuff and get it out of your way.

"It's bad, isn't it?" Shay asked.

Bad. Horrifying. Devastating. Cassie swallowed, determined not to let the tingle in her nose turn into tears. "He's ready to move all his belongings out."

His shirts were what got her through the lonely nights. His scent still lingered in the threads. The soft cotton against her skin helped to create the fantasy he was still there. Still in their marriage bed. What would she do without the constant reminders?

"You're right," Cassie murmured. "I need to play dirty. At least until this is over."

"So, you're going to come to work at Shot of Sin."

Cassie raised her chin and met the mischief in Shay's eyes. "Yep. I'm going to quit my job."

CHAPTER ELEVEN

"*W*asn't it a beautiful day today?"

T.J. raised a brow at Shay's uncharacteristic chipper voice. "Are you high?"

"Nope." She grinned. "Just happy to be alive."

Not high, but clearly up to no good. Nobody should be happy stuck at the Shot of Sin bar on a Thursday night when they'd usually be taking it easy, helping out at Taste of Sin. The two of them had been assigned to a private twenty-first birthday party for a spoiled brat with too much money. None of the kids had manners, and T.J. was certain none of them would be standing once the clock struck midnight. They would either be cut off because they couldn't handle their alcohol consumption or booted from the club for a misdemeanor.

"You know," she started, looking at him thoughtfully, "this place needs more of a woman's touch. There's only so much magic I can add to drown out all the uber-masculine feels."

"The club is fine, Shay." He handed over a raspberry and vodka to a woman who seemed far too young to be legal. "And so is downstairs, and the restaurant, too."

She shrugged. "It was just a thought."

If only she could keep her thoughts to herself, life would be sweet. Well, nowhere near saccharine, but a whole lot better than when she ran her mouth about his personal problems. "I'm going to check on the restaurant. I'll be back later."

He strode around the bar, moving into the small crowd and winced when her voice hit his ears.

"Aren't you meant to be having a meeting with Leo and Brute right about now?"

He turned back to her in confusion. She was focused on her watch, her forehead set in a frown.

"Yep." She met his gaze. "I'm sure Leo said nine pm."

"This is the first I've heard of it."

A firm slap landed on his shoulder before Brute strolled around him. "What's with the meeting? I see your ass too much already."

"Me?" T.J. frowned as Leo walked past on his other side. "I didn't ask for a meeting."

He glanced from Brute's scowl to Leo, who shrugged before diverting his attention to Shay. The bartender was wiping down the counter, pretending to ignore their conversation. He had a sinking feeling she knew more about what was going on than he did. "Shay?"

She raised her gaze, the confidence in her stare wavering as she opened her mouth. "Yeah?"

His hearing honed, blocking out the music of the D.J. and chattering drinkers to the sexy clap of heels approaching from behind him. Leo and Brute glanced over his shoulder, their attention landing on the same spot, their expressions tightening almost imperceptibly.

"Good evening, gentleman."

T.J closed his eyes at the sound of Cassie's voice. He didn't turn, didn't even bother to meet her gaze as her footsteps came to a stop beside him.

"Thank you for meeting me."

"You organized this?" Brute crossed his arms over his chest—his usual defensive stance.

"Oh." Cassie released a gasp and raised her voice to compete with the people dancing around them. "Didn't I write my name at the bottom of the email? Damn it, I could've sworn I did."

Feigning ignorance didn't suit her. She wasn't stupid, and they all knew it. He wanted to call her on it, only he couldn't open his mouth, not without spilling fractured words that would deny the adamant position he was trying to maintain with their divorce.

"I hope you didn't mind me using your email, T.J., I don't have a business account of my own and needed to get in contact with you all as soon as possible."

"Of course not," he ground out, still unable to look at her. He couldn't. He'd begun to live with the pain of being away from her. If he met her sweet stare, he'd have to start all over again. Ripping open barely healed wounds.

"What can we do for you, Cassie?" Leo asked.

She sighed, the feminine sound sinking into his ears and sending an ache through his chest.

"I've lost my job."

T.J.'s heart sank and he finally turned to her. She didn't seem distraught, not when her position at the hotel had been a former source of pride. Instead, she was beautiful, her blonde hair hanging over her shoulders, her black skirt exposing legs he loved entwining with his own. She had the glow of determination in her eyes and confidence showed in her perfect posture.

"With the divorce moving forward and my own income

now non-existent, I've had to rethink my position as silent partner."

His heart was throbbing, pounding. His mind was a mass of thoughts, trying to figure out what was going to fall from her precious lips next.

"I've spent days thinking over my options, and every time I come to the same conclusion. I have no choice but to come work here. At least until I find another job."

Nobody spoke. He wasn't sure if his friends were stunned into silence or waiting for his restraint to crack so they could step in. Either way, he was in hot water, unable to let Cassie nudge her way back into his life, yet also incapable of turning away from her when she needed help.

"What a coincidence," Shay chuckled. "I was telling T.J. a few minutes ago how badly we need more of a feminine touch around here."

He glared at Shay, his blood pressure rising with the smug way she met his stare as she continued to serve people lined along the bar.

"Shay," Leo warned.

"It's not permanent." Cassie's voice was sweet and awkwardly comforting. "I'm already seeking other employment. Things are just slow in my line of work at the moment."

"I'll give you the money," T.J. grated. He'd give her anything, now and after the divorce, she only had to ask. What he couldn't give her was access to his life. Being around her, unable to touch or taste, would tear his already fractured restraint into pieces.

"No," she insisted. "I'm not going to take your money. I need to re-establish my independence."

He remained still. Unwilling to rake a hand through his hair to expose his trembling fingers.

"I think it's a great idea," Shay called from the bar,

striding away to the opposite end to serve the birthday girl. "Welcome to the team."

T.J.'s nostrils flared. Leo wasn't happy either. He was glaring at his girlfriend, his jaw set in a stubborn line, while Brute carried his usual air of disinterest.

"When do you plan on starting?" Leo murmured.

"Actually, I came prepared to learn the ropes tonight. There's been a lot of changes to the club since I was last here, and I thought I could spend the next few hours familiarizing myself."

A tick formed under T.J.'s eye, the nervous twitch causing him to blink. He knew exactly where Cassie wanted to go, and he wouldn't allow it. Not if he couldn't be with her. The Vault of Sin was a place of pleasure, and he could never take her down there and leave her wanting.

It had been his sexual aspiration to introduce her to the club. To show the world how beautiful and responsive she was —the perfect wife. He didn't brag. He didn't boast. But he'd always envisaged the moment when he'd escort her downstairs and the patrons could see for themselves just how lucky he was.

"Maybe another time." Preferably when he was dead and buried. "Go home. Leave us to figure out how to address this."

"I'm afraid you don't understand." She turned to him. "This is my business, too. Anything you need to *figure out* should be done with my involvement."

Brute cleared his throat. "Let's not make this into an issue. I'll show her around. She can work the restaurant bar on slow nights, or help with the books. No big deal."

T.J. kept his gaze on her, wishing he could ignore the silent threat hidden beneath the innocent light blue of her eyes. "She's not going downstairs."

"There's no need to refer to me like I'm not here. We can both be adults about this."

"Can we?" He cocked a brow. She wasn't acting like herself. He'd first noticed it in the way she'd replied to his message on Sunday. He was unfamiliar with her spite. He was used to sweet, nurturing, breathtaking Cassie. The woman before him was someone different, with a smile carved of malice. "You won't go downstairs while you're here."

"This is my business, too. Where I go and what I do is none of your concern, as long as I do my job."

He released a caustic laugh. That's where she was wrong. She'd always be his concern—today, tomorrow and twenty years from now. That was the problem. He couldn't let her go. But he was trying. Every inch of him hurt, every single day, in an effort to let go. If she came to work here, he'd be consumed with the need to be around her. He'd lose his mind. No doubt about it.

He broke away from her gaze and focused on Brute and Leo in turn. "She's not to go down there. Hear me?"

He didn't wait for a reply. He turned and stalked from the Shot of Sin dance floor to head for the upstairs office, as far away from Cassie as possible. There were many things he was capable of right now—madness, mayhem, murder—what he couldn't do was keep pretending he didn't love her with all his heart.

She had too much to lose if they remained together. And even if she didn't know it, he would kill himself trying to make up for the mistakes of his past.

～

Cassie's cheeks ached from pasting the fake smile on her face for the last three hours. She was nervous. Nauseous from treating T.J. badly. Manipulation wasn't something she agreed with, and the only thing keeping her here was the knowledge she'd gotten under his skin.

"I'd like to see downstairs." She waited for her husband's head to jerk up.

She'd been standing at the door to the upstairs office for a few minutes, merely watching him as he sat at the thick oak table, a laptop in front of him. He was lost in thought, not having moved since she'd found his hiding place. His eyes barely blinked as he stared at the screen reflecting its glow back on his handsome face.

"Not tonight." His voice was low, barely reaching her ears.

"Why not? I'd like to see it." She stepped forward, entering the room. He was entirely perfect—his face clean-shaven, his hair styled as usual, his suit flawless. He'd recovered from his misstep on Thursday and was now taking the divorce in stride, when even breathing seemed hard for her. "Brute said he'd be happy to show me around."

His gaze gradually rose to meet hers, his eyes dark with anger. "This isn't up for negotiation."

She scoffed. Who was this man? He'd dictated the terms of their divorce, and even though they were largely made in her favor, she still resented his inability to discuss any of it with her first. Now he was telling her where she could and couldn't go?

"You're right." She kept her tone light, unwilling to let the frustration, pain, anger and grief take over. "I *am* going down there. It isn't up for negot—"

His chair shot back, the rough scrape along the wooden floorboards sending her heart into a rapid beat as he loomed over the desk. "Don't push me, Cassie." He strode for her, his chest rising and falling with labored breaths. "I've said no."

She was scared—that she was pushing him away instead of tugging him forward. That he was beginning to hate her instead of realizing how much he loved her. That the plan was going in the opposite direction and she was digging her own grave. But his anger was far more appealing than his disregard for her existence.

"Why are you against me going down there? That part of the club isn't even open tonight. It's vacant. It's not like I'm married and overseeing a sex club without the presence of my partner."

His jaw clenched, his fists, too. "You said you didn't have a problem with me working down there."

"And I didn't." Not until he'd blindsided her with the end of their marriage. "So, you have no right to say I can't go down there when it's currently unoccupied. When I can't even witness all those images you teased me with. Or experience all the pleasure you once promised. I'm going down there, T.J., whether you like it or not." The more he refused, the more she wanted to push him, hoping he'd break.

"Not now, Cassie."

The way he said her name, the raw savagery, made her throat constrict with sorrow. "Then when?"

Anguish flickered across his features, telling her there would never be a good time. She didn't know what his problem was. It was an empty sex club. Why was he adamant she couldn't enter the sacred walls? Could it be guilt? More misplaced protection? Or did he want to claim the club as his own, trying to keep the taint of his wife out of the sordid area so he could move on easier?

"I don't know."

She gave a sad smile and shrugged. "Well, I think now is the perfect time. And I'm sure I don't need to remind you I'm still part owner, so your permission isn't necessary." She turned and sauntered the few steps to the door. "I'll be going down there with Brute as soon as the private party is finished."

As she reached the threshold, he still hadn't responded,

breaking her heart all over again because he'd stopped fighting so easily. He didn't make sense to her anymore. She couldn't read him. Couldn't predict his thoughts or actions, when once his love had been a reliable strength she could always count on.

She hung her head and entered the hall. No tears formed even though pain consumed her. She was all cried out. She was past waterworks. Tears didn't fix anything. People did. *She* did. So why the heck couldn't she figure out the man she knew better than she knew herself?

"Cass..."

She froze, straightening her shoulders as the muted thump of the downstairs music throbbed around her.

"Don't do this to me," he pleaded. "I've given you the car, the house, the dog. Leave me the Vault. Just give me this one thing."

Her throat tightened, the beat of her heart increasing until the rhythmic pounding became painful. "Don't do this to *you?*" She swung around, hoping the fury in her veins matched the expression on her face. "How dare you? You break my heart, turn my life upside down and expect me to do you favors? And over the same type of establishment that destroyed our marriage? Christ, T.J. Who the hell are you?"

He stood in the doorway, unable to meet her gaze as he opened his mouth to speak.

"No." She raised a hand, cutting him off. "Forget it. I'm going downstairs with Brute. You can have your damn club once the divorce is final. Until then, you better get used to me going wherever the hell I like."

Instead of fighting like she anticipated, he stepped backward, disappearing into the office and closing the door behind him.

Damn him.

The more they fought, the more she questioned what she

was doing. His unfamiliar actions were making her second-guess the marriage they'd once had. Second-guess T.J. in general. Previously, she'd thought he could never taint the memories she had. Now, she wasn't so sure. He was dampening everything. Their love. Their happiness.

Shay was wrong. Being close to him hadn't given her the upper hand. It had resulted in the opposite. Because now she was beginning to believe the divorce may be exactly what they needed. Maybe they were better off alone.

CHAPTER TWELVE

$\mathcal{C}$assie finished stocking bottles of wine into the fridge under the bar and moved to her feet. Shay and Leo were escorting the last of the private party toward the club entrance, while Brute was beside her, clearing away dirty glasses along the counter.

"Are you ready?" she asked.

He didn't glance her way, didn't quit stacking glasses in a long tower to rest against his chest. "Where's T.J.?"

"Still upstairs."

He nodded and continued stacking. "We'll wait a minute."

Cassie frowned. "He's not coming, if that's what you're waiting for."

He cleaned the bar as he went, stacked glasses in one hand, damp cloth in the other, until he reached the dishwasher.

"Do you need a hand?"

"Nope. Leo and Shay can finish up when they come back. I'm just waiting for a minute."

"What are you waiting..." Her words trailed off as a thud

sounded upstairs, then the heavy rhythmic pounding of angered footsteps.

"For that," Brute muttered. "Let's go." He closed the dishwasher and stalked around the bar, leading her toward the locked door at the far side of the club.

"Wait," T.J.'s shout shot down her spine, all the way to her toes.

Brute didn't pause, didn't even glance over his shoulder, so neither did she. T.J. wasn't going to stop her. This was her last hurrah. The final push until she walked away forever.

She sucked in deep breath after deep breath, calming herself as Brute unlocked the heavy padlock securing the entry to the staircase leading to the Vault of Sin.

"Wait," T.J. growled. "I'm coming, too."

Her head snapped around, her eyes greedily eating up the sight of her husband as he strode toward them. He was furious. All that anger and animosity directed right at her. If he was trying to intimidate her, he was failing miserably. Her body had the opposite reaction. Her nipples were pulsing, her throat tight, lips dry.

"Let's get this over with."

Her naïve heart fluttered. Her mind knew his acquiescence didn't mean a thing. It was merely a control measure. But anticipation filled her anyway. This was the first and maybe the last time she'd walk down these stairs with him. What once had been a fantasy was now a broken reality, and she'd take it nonetheless.

Brute swung the door open and waved out an arm for her to proceed. Before her was darkness. She could sense the staircase looming to her left because she knew it was there, yet she had no clue where the light switch was.

"Move," T.J. growled, pushing past her. He flicked on the light, illuminating the staircase she remembered from Thursday night.

Images lined the walls, the hedonistic pictures of sex and foreplay making her pussy throb. The scrape of her thighs against one another as she descended the stairs only made her arousal more potent and the slickness of her sex seep into her panties. She wondered if T.J. would care. Or how he'd react if she told him. Yet telling him scared her. Especially when she now struggled to recognize her husband.

His large frame was tense, his back ramrod straight as he led the way while Brute followed behind her. It could've been intimidating—her angered husband in front, a brutal man at her back—maybe that was their intent. Instead, it awakened fantasies, making her burn all the more to experience the Vault when it was at full capacity, this time without a disguise.

When T.J. reached the bottom step, he flung out his arm and flicked on another set of lights, bringing the entry area into view. She wasn't given a guided tour. T.J. didn't even acknowledge the doors leading to the locker or change rooms. He stormed ahead, moving to the keypad securing the entrance to Vault of Sin at the end of the hall.

He slammed his index finger against four numbers in quick succession and the panel let out a caustic beep. He did it again, slamming harder this time, and earned another beep in return.

"*Fuck.*"

His hand was shaking, his head now hung low with his hair curtaining his eyes. His fragility consumed her, washing away her arousal, replacing it with the need to console. He wasn't just filled with anger. She knew that. Underneath his resentment was pain.

"Want me to do it?" Brute asked.

"Fuck you." T.J. straightened and poised his finger over the panel again. This time, he entered the numbers slower, the same four digits she'd memorized since childhood—one, zero, one, six.

"My birthday," she whispered as the lock released with a click. He may be fighting to push her away now, but back when the club had opened, even after the assault in Tampa, she'd been the first thing on his mind when he'd chosen a security code for the sex club.

He flung the door wide and held it there, peering down at her without emotion as she strolled into the room fighting to hold back a grin. Her first glimpse was different from her recollection. The large screen previously playing porn was black. Silent. The room was bathed in sterile florescent light instead of the dimmer lamps to help set the mood. But it wasn't the Vault she was interested in. It was T.J.'s reaction. He was watching her, not in anger, not in spite, but in pained curiosity.

If only she could bathe him in the praise he deserved for creating such a respectful, reputable environment. She had no delusions that setting up this club had been difficult for him after what they'd gone through. Even though he hadn't been able to bring her down here, a part of her was in every piece of the Vault. She was in the heavy vetting process established to make sure participants were genuine and honest. She was in the classy furniture and clean sheets. She was in the heart of this club, and he'd never be able to take her out.

"This is where the fledglings stay until they feel comfortable playing with the big kids," Brute drawled, squeezing past her.

She inclined her head. "I like the idea."

She continued to watch T.J. from her periphery. His posture was taut, his discomfort visible even from a side glimpse. As she approached, he strode forward, leaving her and Brute alone in the small space.

"Why is he acting like this?" She turned to face Brute.

Her business partner raised a brow. "Maybe because he wants a divorce and you won't let him go."

She snapped her lips shut, refusing to bite back at his heartlessness. There was no empathy in his features. No kindness. No annoyance. Nothing. He was void of emotion.

"You raise a good point." She walked past him, into the main open room of Vault of Sin.

Everything was set out the same as the masquerade party. There was a corner lounge to her left, the bar up ahead with an entrance to the staircase leading to the parking lot hidden around the side. The sex swing still hung in the far corner. There was a king-size bed to her right, and every inch of the room screamed with debauchery, even though there were no writhing bodies.

She pretended to take in her surroundings, while her focus kept returning to T.J. with his back leaned against the bar in between two stools. He was watching her like a hawk. Scrutinizing her perusal, reigniting her arousal.

"I like the sex swing," she announced to no one in particular. "I assume staff get free entry." It was a joke. Her halfhearted chuckle announcing humor that nobody else returned.

T.J.'s nostrils flared, his arms crossing over his chest. "I'd die before I let you participate down here."

She sauntered toward the bar, bridging the space between them, smiling as she did so. "And will you pay me the same respect?" She raised a brow, trying to contain the snarl in her voice. "Or is it already too late?"

His face fell. Undiluted guilt filtered into his features. His eyes, previously harsh with annoyance, filled with devastation. Then, in a blink, it washed away. He schooled his features, straightened and shrugged. "As far as I'm concerned, you're free to do as you wish, Cassie. You just won't be doing it in here."

He met her gaze, her calm, gentle husband nowhere to be seen. Instead, she stared back at a man filled with torment she couldn't soothe. He'd been broken by something. If it wasn't the club in Tampa, she had no clue what. And it scared her to ponder the possibilities.

"Exactly what I thought," she muttered. "You didn't answer the question."

It was harsh to taunt him with guilt he shouldn't feel. Regret he hadn't earned. But she had very few cards up her sleeve, and the knowledge he'd made a mistake on Thursday was one of them.

"I guess I should be happy." She clutched the seats of the stools he stood between, her shoes almost touching his. "Once the divorce is final, I'll be able to get back to exploring all those things you promised me."

He broke eye contact, his jaw ticking. His chest began to rise and fall, his chin jutting to fight off her attack. She didn't move back, didn't leave his personal space. She couldn't. This harsh side of him did things to her belly, and places much lower. If only he'd succumb to his desire for her. She knew it was there, hidden under his fear.

"I wish you all the best with finding what you need." His words were like a steel blade—lethal, sterile, cold. Deep down, she knew he didn't mean it. He couldn't. But her strength to push wavered under his callousness.

They were playing a game. Each of them shoving at the other, waiting for the first one to crack. He would either succumb to his need for her and revoke the poor excuse for a divorce, or she would buckle under his heartlessness, too hurt to keep fighting him.

"Do you mind if we pause the tour so I can use the bathroom?" She couldn't maintain the strong façade much longer. She needed privacy. A few moments to regroup before she came back swinging.

"No problem." His focus narrowed on her, his curiosity seeing straight through her. He knew he was winning the war. And by the barely visible pity in Brute's eyes, he did, too.

❧

*T.*J. watched her disappear into the room leading to the bathrooms. He'd grown weak, his gaze tracking her every movement, his feelings for her shoving to the forefront again.

"She sure knows her way around for someone who's never been down here before," Brute drawled.

T.J. tore his attention from the doorway and scowled. "What do you mean?"

Brute shrugged, acting as if his words weren't a bombshell. "I sure as hell didn't show her where the bathrooms are."

Panic washed over him. "She couldn't..." It would have been impossible for her to get into the Vault. "You handle all entry information. How could she have been down here without you knowing?"

Brute narrowed his gaze. "Is that accusation I hear in your tone?"

No. It was fury. How the fuck had his wife gotten into Vault of Sin without his approval? The how, what, where and when assailed him. Was it recently? Had it been all those months ago when the Vault first opened? Or maybe a few nights ago at the masquerade party, hiding under a disguise to watch him disrespect their marriage vows.

"When?" he asked through clenched teeth. "How could this happen?"

His mouth dried as he tried to figure it out. The Vault was locked when not in use. Dead-bolted. On event nights, not only did the downstairs entrance have a digital alarm, the upstairs door and parking lot entrance were both manned by

115

security guards. If she was callous enough to try and attend a night the Vault was open, she would've had to go through the approval process—photos, ID, approval at the door. It was impossible.

"Maybe she took a wild stab at where they were." He glanced at Brute in hope.

His friend raised a brow, not needing to back up his disbelief with anything other than his confident stare.

Fuck. "It had to be Shay." She'd been a pain in his ass since the news of his divorce.

Brute narrowed his focus to a glare. "Accusing Shay without evidence is going to land you in a world of hurt."

As if he wasn't there already. "For her sake, I hope I'm wrong."

Shay was a friend, but above all else, she was an employee. One that seemed more committed to gossip than her duties to their business. She'd asked one too many questions about his divorce. Had followed him around like gum stuck to his shoe. And when Cassie had showed up tonight, Shay hadn't been surprised at all, as if they'd planned the reunion together.

"Hold on a goddamn minute." He turned toward the room his wife had disappeared into. "Shay has never met Cassie before. Why the hell did they seem familiar with one another when Cassie turned up tonight?"

Brute's lips twitched slightly as he shrugged again.

Motherfucker. Something was going on, and it was about time T.J. put a stop to it.

"You better not be involved." He pointed a menacing finger toward Brute's chest and stormed away, hell-bent on finding the answers he couldn't live without.

CHAPTER THIRTEEN

*C*assie was washing her hands in the basin when the bathroom door flung open, hitting the wall with a deafening crack. She turned, startled by a remembered sense of fear from a similar situation, and stared at the fury in T.J.'s eyes as he loomed in the doorway.

"You've been down here before."

She snapped her gaping mouth shut and schooled her expression. *Breathe.* She broke the words down in her mind, hoping to convince herself they were spoken in jealousy, not hatred. "I don't know what you're talking about."

His nostrils flared and his large frame inched forward, for the first time coming toward her with menace. "You gave yourself away."

She turned back toward the basin, lowering her head as she calmly grabbed the hand towel and dried her fingers. "I gave what away?"

He growled, the deep rumble of his chest caressing her ears. He came up behind her, grabbed the towel and threw it back onto the counter. "Look at me."

She swallowed, raising her focus to the mirror and the furious man staring back at her. For a second, she was scared, not of him, but of how their marriage was turning into more of a mangled wreck with each passing second. Soon it would be unsalvageable. Soon all hope would be lost.

He grabbed her wrist and spun her to face him. Although he was angry as hell, his grip was in contrast, a light caress, a loving brush of fingers. She turned to him, glimpsed the sadness in his eyes right before his gaze fell to where they touched, and he dropped his hold.

Emotions flickered across his features—heartache, yearning, confusion, before finally morphing back to anger. "Answer me," he snarled.

She scoffed. "From my understanding, all you've done is fling accusations at me. I've yet to be asked a question." She stepped into him and raised her chin so they were almost eye to eye. "And even if you were demanding answers from me, you have no right anymore. I'm no longer your concern."

"Don't play with me, Cass." He stepped into her, thigh to thigh, menacingly close.

She'd never been immune to his dominance. Outside of the bedroom, they were a regular couple. Scratch that. Outside of the bedroom, they were an enviable couple, their love evident to anyone who witnessed them together. Behind closed doors, the parallels of their relationship changed. He was no longer the protector. He was the predator. The man with an insatiable need for her, a passion so carnal she woke up in a sweat from mere dreams of it.

"I can't stand seeing you this way." His nose scrunched in distaste. "Spite doesn't look pretty on you."

Spite? *Spite*. Could he not see she was fighting for her life here? For his love?

"Yeah?" She raised a brow in defiance. "Well, being a coward doesn't look favorably on you either."

"I'm not a coward, Cass."

"Hmm?" She narrowed her gaze. "Then what would you call it? You're running away from a perfect marriage. You're hiding from something you can't even tell me about. If that's not cowardice, I don't know what is."

"There's a lot you don't know."

"Because you won't tell me." Her voice turned to a plea.

"It's better this way. I need you to come to terms with that."

"No. You need to come to terms with me not giving up on us." Her tone lacked conviction. Her heart, too. She couldn't take much more of this. Fighting for a man who no longer wanted to be fought for. Battling for a cause that had already been lost. "Until I have all the answers, I can't give up. I need closure." She stepped into him, resting her forearms against his chest. "Tell me why you need this divorce. Tell me what changed if it wasn't that night in Tampa."

She ran her tongue over her bottom lip, unable to stop herself when he was so close. Her mouth ached for him. All she needed was a kiss. A connection. She'd convince him to stay from the slightest contact.

"You still desire me." She didn't break their stare. "I think you always will."

"You're right. But my attraction to you was never in question."

She balked at his honesty. "Then what is it? Don't you love me anymore?"

Her fingers clung to his shirt, her gaze raking his features, scouring for answers. She was inching closer to where she needed to be. If she knew what she was fighting against, she could better equip herself. She'd no longer be battling in the dark.

"Tate, *please* tell me."

His gaze softened, his lips parted as if poised to speak.

Then the shield went down, his forehead scrunched in annoyance, and he stepped back with a derisive laugh. "You almost had me."

He shook his head, ran a hand over the darkened stubble of his chin. "But let's get back to the real reason I'm in here, shall we?" Her heart dropped at the returned venom in his tone. "Tell me, Cassie. When did you come to the Vault without me?"

~

ell. How the fuck had this turned back to him? He couldn't think straight around her. She was confusing him. Changing the subject without him noticing. He hadn't come in here to succumb to the emotional plea in her eyes. He'd come for answers.

"How did you get in?" He attempted to act in control even though he was backtracking, stepping away from her.

She huffed. "I guess we both have questions that won't get answered."

The way she focused on him, intent, powerful, made him drown in the sparkling gorgeousness of her conviction. She had unending faith in them. In their love. And fuck, it was tearing him apart. He wanted to tell her, to announce the truth and let her know this divorce wasn't what he wanted.

It was what he needed—to protect her.

He'd changed her. Shaped a beautifully innocent woman into a skillful seductress because of his wants and desires. He'd driven her to be curious about a place like the filthy establishment in Tampa. But that was only half of his problem. The rest was out of his control. There was so much she didn't know, and telling her would only inflict more pain.

"I guess we're done here." She paused for a moment, waiting for words he couldn't find. With an overly dramatic flick of her hair over her shoulder, she turned on her heel and sauntered out of the bathroom, leaving him to sink into infatuation.

He couldn't help it. Couldn't fight it. No matter how much time they spent apart, he'd always want her. Need her. Beg to be between her heavenly thighs, tearing murmurs of adoration from her lips. Even just to hold her. To comfort. He'd give all their years together if they could start again. He had no control over his body's reaction to Cassie. His palms itched to touch, his lips ached at the thought of a kiss.

There had never been anything more mesmerizing than the love and affection he'd once glimpsed in her eyes. Yet here, now, the spark of determination he'd seen burning inside her was like a physical caress over his cock.

He all but jogged from the bathroom, yanking the door open with too much force. "How did you get down here?" His voice was loud, almost a yell. He still needed answers. Even more so, he needed her proximity.

She stopped at the foot of the large bed in the center of the room and slid a hand on her hip. "I followed you down here, remember?"

"You know I'm not talking about tonight." He lumbered toward her, clenching his fists at his sides to stop from reaching for her. "Tell me when you've been down here before."

"Or what?" She cocked a brow. "What are you going to do if I don't tell?"

He growled his frustration, the rumble burning from his chest all the way up his throat. "I already know the answer. I could tell by your lack of surprise when you walked in here tonight. I'd just been too distracted until now to pick up on it. There's no point denying the truth, Cass. I know you've been down here."

Her lips tilted in a seductive curve. "Maybe."

"Who let you in?"

The curve of her lips increased. "That's not your concern anymore, remember?"

Jealousy, thick and rich, pulsed through his veins. "Cassie." Her name vibrated from his lips in a lethal combination of anger and anguish.

"Tate," she mimicked.

"When?" The bed was right here. At his side. A taunting possibility that he could throw her on the mattress and tie her down until he'd sated himself inside her addictive body. "Did a staff member show you around? Was it Travis? Shay? Or was it during a party night?"

"Why do you want to know so badly?" She was enjoying this. The excitement was in her eyes, the kick of her lips. He was revealing his cards. Showing her he still cared. "Why, T.J.? You made it clear you no longer love me."

He squeezed his eyes shut, unwilling to fall into her trap. He wanted to deny it, to explain exactly how much her love meant to him. But he couldn't afford to take another retreating step tonight.

"You entered the club without my knowledge. I want to know how." He opened his eyes and peered down at her, taking the final step between them. She had a hold of him. Every limb, every breath. He could no longer stand the thought of her down here without him. The need to know burned through his veins. The images of her amongst the club patrons was torture.

"Please." He glided his fingers over her jaw, gently grabbed her chin and savored the way her eyes fluttered closed. "You're fucking gorgeous, Cassie. I can only imagine the impact you had on the regulars if you came down here while it was open."

He ran his thumb over her chin, grazing the sensitive skin

just below her mouth. "Was it, sweetheart? Did you come here to play? Did Brute see you? Leo?"

She was falling under his spell, her lips parting in need. Problem was, he was equally consumed with desire. His cock was throbbing, pounding in an incessant beat to match his pulse.

He ran a hand through her loose hair and placed the other on her hip, ascending, climbing higher until his palm was almost at the curve of her breast. "Tell me," he whispered. "When were you down here?"

She shook her head, denying him her thoughts, but not her body. Her head leaned into his grasp, her chest into his, the warmth of her abdomen scorching his cock.

He was slipping out of lucidity, his head now filled with thoughts of pleasure, his body lost to the possibility of release. He leaned in, brushed his lips over the perfection of the smooth skin below her ear and breathed in her perfume.

"Tell me." He was no longer sure what he was asking for. Couldn't remember why he was even here, apart from the need to have her.

Her hands came to rest on his pecs. The greedy scratch of her nails above his shirt drove him insane with want. It had been over twelve months since he'd paid homage to her body. More than 365 days. An eternity.

His mind knew that was way too long. His cock did, too. It was his heart, the painful ache in his chest that tainted the moment, reminding him he'd made the choice to give up this pleasure. He couldn't succumb under the weight of attraction.

But he'd started this for a reason. He still needed answers. Sleeping at night wouldn't be an option if he didn't find out when she'd been here and what she'd done. He pulled back, waited until her eyes blinked open, before he wove her hair around his fist, making it impossible for her to move. "I need to know."

"And I need you." She trailed her fingertips down his chest, over his stomach to the crotch of his pants. Her hand palmed his cock, releasing a needy little moan as she did it.

He snarled, hating how weak she made him, fighting the burn of attraction as she nuzzled her nose against his. "*Tell me.*"

He didn't wait for an answer he knew wasn't coming. Instead, he smashed his mouth against hers and gripped the back of her head to hold her tightly. He parted her lips with his tongue and ground his erection into her.

He could feel her everywhere—against his chest, in his mind, through his soul.

"*Tell me,*" he growled into her mouth.

She whimpered, her body going languid against him. Her lips were the most delicate silk, her scent an intoxicating blend of everything sweet and vulnerable in the world. She gripped his shirt and pulled it from his waistband, brushing her fingers against his skin like a branding iron.

His need for answers became lost in the urgency to have her. *Twelve months*, he kept repeating to himself. He'd done without this for twelve months. How had he lived? How had he breathed?

He lifted her, placed her on the clean sheets of the bed in the middle of the room and then strode for the door, slamming it shut with a hard shove of his trembling hand.

When he turned to her, she was on her back, resting against her elbows, her body a vision he'd been starved of. He wanted to make it right, to turn off the fluorescent lights and bathe her in the warm glow of the lamp, but this wasn't about setting a mood or deepening her already infallible appeal. This was about finding answers. It was. It really, really was.

If only he could focus.

He stormed for her, not stopping until his knees hit the mattress, jolting the bed frame. "Tell me," he demanded. "When were you here?"

She frowned, breaking the glazed look of arousal. "I guess this was a mistake." She pushed to a seated position, her body turning briefly to the opposite side of the bed in an attempt to flee.

Like hell. He lunged for her, caught her around the waist and dragged her back to the center of the mattress. When he released her this time, something new twinkled in her eyes. Something fierce and deliciously naughty. Something he'd never seen from Cass before.

He lunged for her again, this time her mouth, slamming his lips into hers with enough force to steal the breath from her lungs. She clung to him, digging her fingertips into his shoulders, running a hand through his hair. He was lost, delirious, inching closer to being sated.

He parted her legs with a shove of his knee and sank his body between her thighs, pinning her to the bed. She didn't protest, didn't deny him, yet when he pulled back, the look she gave him was lethal. A warning he was sure he'd regret not adhering to in the near future.

With his pelvis holding down her lower body, he reached for the bedside dresser and removed a scarf from the drawer. She licked her lips as he slanted over her, her gaze tracing his movements as he tied her left and then her right wrist to the wrought-iron bedhead.

She was a sight. Splayed for his gratification. A goddess at his mercy. *Exquisite.* All he needed was her clothes on the floor and her legs parted with restraints, then she would be perfect.

He cascaded one hand over her body—down her arm, over the curves of her breasts to the softness of her waist. "I could touch you for hours."

She bucked her hips, pulsing her abdomen into him, making his fingers itch to go lower. "Yet you haven't in months."

He ignored her, unable to give her a response that wouldn't incite self-loathing. He'd vowed to stay away, to let her move on. More importantly, he'd promised himself not to succumb to his desires, not wanting to give her hope... And now look where he was.

Fuck. He needed to get out of here. *Now.* "When were you here, Cass?"

She whimpered, undulating her hips against his. "Kiss me." Her voice was breathy—a seductive plea.

He lowered his head to her neck, hiding his pain from view. There was no doubt she thought this was about lust, and, yes, he was burning to have her. But what kept him here was fear. The panic that she was curious enough to attend a sex club without him. That she could walk into another predator's trap in the future if he wasn't there to look after her. And it was jealousy, too. So much goddamn jealousy he wanted to cry out at the pain of it.

There was no other man for her. There couldn't be.

Not now. Not ever.

He brushed his mouth against her neck, her jaw, her cheek. Each touch resulted in a tiny whimper from her lips, and a harsh pulse of blood to his cock. "I suppose I can't blame you for your curiosity." He lavished her with delicate kisses. "I'm just disappointed I wasn't here to witness the first time you came to the Vault."

Devastated was more accurate.

Her eyes were closed, her hands gripping the scarf woven around her palms. He licked the seam of her lips, teased her tongue with his own. She was so receptive, her body rising to meet the glide of his hand as it travelled lower, over her thigh to the hem of her short skirt.

He didn't want to go this far. He'd die a million deaths getting over this. Only she felt too good. Too right.

"God, how I've missed this body." He hadn't meant to say it aloud. Her curves did crazy things to him. She was the perfect fit, a flawless woman in every sense of the word. He closed his eyes as the tips of his fingers reached her panties, the heat of her sex so close to his touch. "Tell me, gorgeous. Did you come here to see me?"

She whimpered again, this time tilting her head to demand a kiss he wouldn't give.

"You can tell me." He was struggling to find the strength to speak. The power to stop. He wanted to shuck his pants and drive into her, knowing full well her pussy would be dripping wet for him.

"Yes." She nodded, straining against her restraints. "I was here."

He froze, every nerve tense, every muscle taut. "When?" He spoke even though his throat threatened to close over.

"Does it matter?" she panted.

He growled, his frustration barely contained. The tips of his fingers ran through the brief patch of hair at the apex of her thighs, his touch stopping on the swollen nub just beneath. "Everything matters," he grated into her ear. "Tell me everything."

She shook her head, her hands pulling tighter against the scarf.

He flicked her clit, once, twice, gaining sadistic satisfaction every time she whimpered. The need for her ran heavy through his veins, pulsing with undeniable intent. He had to pleasure her. To bring her to climax like he had so many times before.

"I was here last week."

He stopped breathing. His vision blurred. "At the masquerade party?"

She mewled, nodding.

Vertigo assailed him, and he sank the arm he rested on deeper into the bed to keep him stable while his fingers clung to the sheet. He forced his other hand to continue stroking her clit, denying himself the need to flee before he knew every little detail.

"Were you with someone?"

She opened her eyes, the arousal flickering under the scrutiny of her narrowed gaze. "Yes." The word was emphatic, confident, shooting an arrow through his chest.

"Tell me who, Cass." He couldn't control the steel in his tone. He would kill the man. Maim him, at the very least. "Who were you with?"

Her features softened, the caring, sweet woman he knew came shining through. She leaned forward, then fell back and huffed in frustration over the restraints. She snaked out her tongue, moistening kiss-darkened lips. "I was with the man I love."

Fuck. Her words were like dynamite, blowing him to pieces. He slid back, moving from the bed, unwilling to believe what her words implied.

"I was with you," she continued.

"No." His heart pumped at the speed of a freight train. His mind flashed images with vivid clarity. The new member —the woman with black hair and brown eyes. *Jesus Christ.* She'd gone to a lot of trouble to trick him.

"Yes," she whispered. "You kissed *me*, T.J. You were attracted *to me.*"

Fucking hell. He'd died ten times over from guilt because of her. Yet he'd known. Somehow. There was no way he could've kissed someone else. His subconscious had known it was her. Even under the disguise.

"I knew you still loved me," she announced with conviction. "Thursday night was proof of that. You couldn't resist. Just like you can't now. We weren't meant to be apart, T.J."

He ignored her, wiping a hand down his face as he began to pace. "How did you get in?"

She tugged at her restraints and huffed. "Can you untie me?"

"*How*, Cassie?"

She flopped back against the pillows. "Fake ID."

He stopped pacing, nodded and succumbed to defeat. He'd received the answers he needed to sleep at night. He'd also received a reprieve from a small part of his guilt. Now it was time to leave.

He strode for the head of the bed, focusing on her restraints instead of the glimmer of hope in her eyes. He was a fucking bastard. A coward, like she'd accused earlier. He leaned down and kissed the smooth skin of her wrist, right above the scarf.

"I know you still love me." She reached for his face.

He pulled away, unable to withstand the affection in her touch. This was it. The final blow that would make her stop doubting that their marriage was over. He needed to convince her to move on. And unfortunately, he knew exactly how to do it.

"The affect you had was desire." He straightened to his full height, glancing down at her with what he hoped was a convincing look of pity. "Nothing more."

The lie stung, and each word he spoke crumpled her determined features into a mass of heart-wrenching anguish.

"I don't believe you."

A part of him cheered that she knew him so well. The rest of him died under the need to push harder. He shrugged, giving her a look that belied the guilt assailing him. "I'm not going to waste time mourning our marriage. I'm moving on. I suggest you do the same."

Her face paled, the final blow hitting its mark. He turned, unable to see her like this. Unable to withstand it when he was the one tearing her apart. He strode for the door, each step away from her bringing more agony.

She wouldn't recover from this. He knew it, because he wouldn't recover either.

CHAPTER FOURTEEN

"*T*.J." Cassie screamed at the door her husband had closed behind him and sank back into the pillows. Humiliation assailed her, dragging tears from her eyes to trail down the side of her face.

He wasn't coming back to untie her.

She was alone. Sobbing. Trying in vain to fight herself free of the silk scarf he'd tied her hands in. Her skin already burned from the friction, and the pain came nowhere near what she felt inside her chest.

The far-off beat of footsteps approached, the click of a door releasing and the squeak as it was pushed open an inch.

"T.J.?"

"You decent?" *Brute*. Perfect. Her night couldn't get any worse.

"Not really," she muttered. Her nose was a running mess, her skirt raised to her hips, displaying her silken underwear. The only saving grace was the panties that covered her intimate parts...the same parts that still throbbed from her husband's touch.

He'd never had a problem arousing her. He'd always made

it his mission to make her come before him. Usually, more than once. Walking away while she was wild with need was a sign she finally needed to sit back and listen to. Her husband was gone, and the man who'd taken his place wasn't afraid of making her feel worthless and dirty.

"Too bad." Brute shoved into the room, his features schooled, not showing shock or disgust at how she was tied to the bed, her cheeks tear-streaked, her clothes and hair disheveled. "Looks like you had fun."

She glared at him as he came to the side of the bed and untangled the scarf on her right wrist. "Yeah," she grated. "It's like fucking Disneyland in here."

He paused, at her uncharacteristically bad language or the crack in her voice, she wasn't sure. Her wrist fell free with the release of the material and she looked to the far side of the room, unable to stand his impassive scrutiny.

"You took a risk by pushing him." Brute made his way to the other side of the bed. "Unfortunately, it backfired."

She glared straight ahead, tugged down the hem of her skirt with one hand while he approached her other wrist.

"Are you going to give up now? I assume it would be better to maintain some sort of friendship, or whatever you normal people have, instead of being unable to communicate at all."

Neither option had been acceptable before she'd come downstairs. Now she wasn't sure if never seeing T.J. again was such a bad idea. He'd tainted memories she'd never thought could be spoiled. He was not only destroying their future, he was contaminating their past.

"I couldn't believe he'd give up on us." She wiggled her wrist free as he loosened the scarf. "I had to fight for what we had."

He inclined his head, his expression devoid of care. She would've denied he had compassion at all if it wasn't for the cotton handkerchief he pulled from his trouser pocket and thrust in her direction.

She blew her nose and dabbed at her cheeks. "I was here the night of the masquerade party. He kissed me."

"You think I didn't know you were here?" He gave a harsh laugh. "Nobody passes through those doors without me knowing. Although, you did a good job on the fake ID, I wasn't entirely convinced it was you until you showed up."

"You knew?" Her voice rose. "Why didn't you say something? Why didn't you tell T.J.?"

He shrugged. "It wasn't my place. You obviously went to great lengths to gain entry to the club, and I had no doubt it was to try to win him back. And besides, I wanted to see if you had the balls to show up. I never thought you were the devious type."

He settled onto the bed at her side, reached for her with a furrowed brow and swept the tear-soaked hair from her cheek, as if the gentle gesture was foreign. "He doesn't want to hurt you." The words were barely audible, barely believable from such a harsh man. "We all know that. This is his way of protecting you. Let him. That's all he has left."

She growled and pulled away from his touch. "Protecting me from what?"

"The past." His lips tilted. "The present." His grin increased. "The future."

"Is this a game to you?" she snapped, sliding from the bed.

"No." He stood, facing her from the far side of the mattress. "Kinda feels like I'm in an X-rated soap opera, though."

She scowled, seeing his actions for what they were—a diversion. He'd shown too much sympathy, and now he was making up for it by being an asshole. Hiding the softer side of himself in an effort to protect his vulnerability.

"I feel sorry for you." She did. She really did. He was cold.

Heartless. Lacking the ability to step out on a limb because he was too scared to be hurt. "You must be lonely."

"Lonely? Why? I have everything I need—money, prestige and innumerable women at my disposal."

"You don't have love."

He scoffed. "Does it even exist?"

It was her turn to look at him with pity. "Sure it does. I should know. I experienced it with T.J. for years."

She gave him a sad smile in farewell and then strode for the door. Once she reached the threshold, she paused, realizing she was unable to leave without making her way back up those stairs toward her husband.

"Need me to get something for you?" Brute spoke over her shoulder.

She sagged and nodded. "Please." She needed to leave out the back entrance. To scamper away like the dirty vermin T.J. had turned her into. "My purse and keys are under the main bar."

Brute squeezed past her, doing her bidding without a falter in his step. He was probably happy to see the back of her, too. The secured door clunked in the distance, cocooning her in silence. She sucked in a breath, waiting, the minutes ticking by like slow, dreary days. She memorized her surroundings, strolling around the furniture, brushing her fingers along the sofa backs.

She refused to glance toward the mirror behind the bar. Her reflection would tell her what her aching heart already knew—it was over. There was no more will to fight. All hope was lost.

In a few weeks, she would be single. Alone. Broken. As if she could shatter any more than she already had.

The swoosh of the door opening startled her, and she made her way toward the newbie area.

"This it?" Brute asked, holding out her purse and keys.

"Yeah." She nodded, taking her belongings from his hand before wrapping her arms around her chest. "I guess this is goodbye."

He pressed his lips together, the harshness of his features becoming more sterile as he frowned down at her. "I guess so."

She held in a caustic laugh and turned on her heel. A Shot of Sin had been a big part of her marriage when it first opened. Now it would be a memory. A brief flicker of remembrance.

"Cass, wait."

She glanced over her shoulder, to the steely expression that hadn't faltered. The only difference was Brute's stance, his arms were raised, held open in front of him.

She pivoted back to him, frowning.

"Come on," he growled. "This is more uncomfortable for me than it is for you."

His discomfort brought a brief smile to her lips. "You're a confusing man, Bryan."

He rolled his eyes and stepped forward, engulfing her in a hug. For a long time, they simply held each other, her head on his shoulder, his arms around her back.

"I've always admired T.J.," he spoke into her hair. "He puts himself last, no matter what the situation. And he's far too kind for his own good. He'd rather push you away and torture himself in the process than expose you to something hurtful. I envy his selflessness."

Cassie pushed back from Brute's chest and looked him in the eye. "Right now, I loathe it."

"Understandable." He inclined his head. "But even though he's acting this way, deep down I think he'd want you to know your pain is killing him."

"I thought you didn't get involved in personal matters."

She gave a halfhearted grin, unable to keep it plastered on her face for longer than a few seconds.

"I guess I'm a sucker for a damsel in distress."

"No." She shook her head, sliding from his embrace. "You've got a big heart. You're just too afraid to show it."

"Nah. I really don't." He glanced toward the bar, denying her his gaze. "If you leave out the back door, I'll lock it behind you."

She wanted to laugh at the abrupt change in conversation. Instead, she thumped his shoulder with her purse, lightening the mood. "I'll see you around, big guy."

He nodded, his features returning to their emotionless state. "Look after yourself."

"Will do." She headed for the staircase leading to the parking lot, ignoring the impending breakdown she could feel pressing on her shoulders. The time had come to move on. No more second-guessing. No more trying to fight an unidentifiable opponent. Her marriage was over. And after tonight, she was determined to move on.

~

T.J. leaned against the wall beside the upstairs entrance to the Vault, waiting for Brute to return. As soon as the door opened, he straightened, watching as his business partner strode for the bar.

"Is she gone?" His voice echoed through the empty room, taunting him.

"Yep." Brute's tone was too blasé for T.J.'s liking. "For good."

Fuck. He ran a hand over his face and tilted his head to the ceiling. "Is she okay?"

"You don't want to hear how she is." Brute continued

136

across the dance floor, heading for Shay and Leo who stood behind the bar.

"Yeah, I do." T.J. pushed off the wall. "Tell me."

Brute swung around. "She's fucked. Is that what you want to hear?" He threw his hands up in the air and let them drop to his sides. "You've broken her. She's done. Gone. Congratulations."

"Jesus," Shay whispered.

"You stay the fuck out of this." T.J. stormed for the bar, pointing a threatening finger in her direction as his mental stability splintered. "It's your fault she was here."

Shay balked at his vicious tone. "What—"

"Have I disrespected you in some way? Was this retaliation for something I've done? Or were you just being a heartless, nosy bitch, thinking you knew better because I'm merely a male and have no clue what it's like to feel?"

The words flowed from his mouth like he was stuck in an out-of-body experience. They were his thoughts that never should've been spoken. His torment that should've remained his own.

Her mouth opened, closed. She glanced to her left, to Leo at her side, before returning to face him. "It was neither. I—"

"You encouraged her to come tonight, didn't you?"

"I...I..." Her shoulders fell and she gave a brief nod. "I know you love her. I thought the two of you could work things out if you spent some time together."

"Fucking hell, Shay," Brute muttered.

"It's not her fault." Leo came around the bar. "Her heart was in the right place. She was only trying to help."

"Well, she didn't. She made me spit in the face of my marriage. And I want to know what the fuck you plan to do about it. She can't work here anymore. I want her gone."

"That's the pain talking," Leo growled. "Shay's far more than an employee to us, and you know it."

T.J. raised his chin, refusing to agree.

"Look, you're pissed. We know that." Brute strode around the back of the bar and pulled a can of Scotch and dry from the fridge. "But Cass is out of your hair now. She's moving on. You've got what you wanted. Don't go blaming anyone else for something you put into motion."

T.J. clenched his jaw, breathing heavily through his nose in an effort to keep the hateful words in his chest. It *was* his fault. He *was* to blame.

"What was I meant to do?" he asked. "I can't tell her the truth. It will kill her."

"What *is* the truth, T.J.?" Shay asked.

Leo winced and shook his head, but the silent protest wasn't enough to stop the words that inched up T.J.'s throat. "Six months ago, the man who assaulted her was charged with a brutal rape. The woman almost died."

Shay gasped. "Cassie doesn't know?"

"No," he grated. "And I don't plan on telling her either. She would blame herself when it isn't her fault."

It was his.

If only he hadn't taken her to that sex club. If only he would've listened to his gut and not allowed her to walk from his side to use the bathroom. She never would've been assaulted and he wouldn't have the guilt of two tortured women weighing down his shoulders.

"Then don't tell her...but you can't divorce her because of this either," Shay begged.

"You expect me to hide it from her for the rest of my life?" He glared. "I *love her*, Shay. I'd do anything for her. But what I won't do is create a marriage based on lies. She deserves more than me. She deserves more than a man who would put her in that sort of position."

He'd only found out about the charges because he'd

employed an investigator to do some digging. Almost six months to the day after that night in the club, he'd received an email with images attached. A twenty-six-year-old, shy and beautiful, had been dragged into a car. She hadn't stood a chance.

"Cassie currently thinks this divorce is hard," he continued. "If she found out what this man could've done to her, or what could've been avoided if only we'd gone to the police, she won't recover. I can't do that to her."

He ground his teeth together and focused a lethal stare on Shay. "And I won't allow you to shove your nose into our business and risk her finding out just so you can push your own agenda.

"I'm sorry." Her face crumpled. "I didn't know."

"Sorry doesn't cut it." *Fucking hell*. The things he'd said to Cassie downstairs... The things he'd done. Even God couldn't forgive him for betraying her like that.

"The offer to fuck him up is still on the table." Brute drank from the can, not even bothering to focus his full attention on the way T.J.'s life was ending.

"No. Thank you," T.J. grated. "He was caught and prosecuted. Once he was sent to jail, the story died, and that's how I want it to stay."

"He deserves some form of retaliation."

T.J. inclined his head. "Yes, but at the risk of Cassie finding out? I'd prefer him to rot in his cell."

Shay turned to Leo. "You knew about this?"

"Yeah. Since the masquerade party."

"But, T.J., you love her so much." Her voice rose. "You can't leave her."

He'd spent months trying to determine if he could live a lie just to stay with Cassie. Counseling hadn't helped. He either had to tell the truth and watch her suffer through the consequences, knowing with each passing day that he was to blame. Or he could leave and allow her to find a brighter future with someone else.

"There's no other option."

Brute slammed his can on the counter and pulled another from the fridge. "I still think that bastard needs to suffer."

"And you think I don't? He's in jail. What's done is done." Cassie was gone. He'd pushed her to her breaking point and doubted she'd have the heart to fight back.

"Then I suggest we let it go." Leo crossed his arms over his chest. "Let *her* go."

Words were so easily spoken. It was the pain they inflicted that made it hard to breathe. "Yeah, just dust that shit off, right?"

As if it would ever be that easy.

Leo snarled. "Look, we're trying to be here for you, but you're making it fucking hard."

"*Leo,*" Shay chastised and made her way onto the dance floor. "I made a huge mistake, and I'm incredibly sorry. I never would've placed Cassie in this situation if I knew. Please forgive me."

T.J. looked away. He didn't want to hurt her. It *was* the pain, the anger and the desperation making him volatile. "I can't even forgive myself right now."

She nodded. "Then tell me what I can do to help. I know you have to pick up your belongings on Sunday. Let me do that for you."

To hell with that. He'd do it himself. He was becoming accustomed to seeing his wife pained beyond recognition. Nobody else deserved to experience her anguish like he did. "No, it's okay."

Misguided or not, these people were his friends, and he was punishing them for something that was his fault. "This is my mistake. Let's just pretend like tonight didn't happen."

And the years with Cassie were only a dream. "I'm going to go home. I'll see you all tomorrow."

Silence followed him as he walked from Shot of Sin. Silence and mourning. He'd done the right thing...maybe not in the right way, but protecting Cassie from the past had been his aim, and he'd achieved that. Now all he had to do was live with the consequences.

CHAPTER FIFTEEN

*C*assie spent three days in hiding. She didn't answer the door when Jan came over, or pick up the phone when Shay called. She didn't even turn on the television to let the outside world in.

Instead, she packed T.J.'s things. Piece by piece, she placed her husband's belongings into empty boxes. She could've thrown them on the front lawn, giving him a taste of retaliation, but she wasn't convinced he'd even care anymore. She no longer knew how he would react, or if he was even going to show up to claim what she'd packed.

She hadn't spoken to him since she'd run from the club on Thursday night. Hours later, she'd started removing his things from her life. The process had been cathartic. Each item of clothing, pair of shoes and personal object had received a silent goodbye to the memories they held.

His wedding tux had been the hardest. She'd unzipped the clothing protector, flattened the familiar outfit on the bed and lain on top of it. With softly falling tears, she'd closed her eyes, wrapping her arms around the waist of the coat, pretending she was back there. On their special day. Speaking vows of love and commitment.

She was stronger now though. All that remained of T.J. were stacked boxes at her door. She'd blocked him from her mind. Pushed him from her heart. And would proceed to carry on with her chin held high.

But as Bear began to bark from the backyard, she wasn't sure who she'd been kidding. This was it. There was no reason for him to come back after today. There was nothing to keep him here.

She sucked in a deep breath and yanked the front door open.

"T.J.," she greeted.

He gave her an awkward smile. "Hi, Cass."

She broke eye contact, unable to stand the familiar man who acted like a stranger. "I've packed your things and stacked the boxes inside the door. There's a few more in the dining room."

"You didn't have to do that."

No, she didn't. She owed him nothing. "I'll leave you to it."

He inclined his head, his face solemn as he leaned inside and grabbed the first heavy box from the stack.

He walked away with too much ease. She didn't understand it. Couldn't contemplate how a man who'd once claimed to love her with all his heart could find it so easy to cut ties. But she wasn't going to think about that anymore. Nope. Not even once.

She strode for the back of the house, breathing through the pain overtaking her lungs. She refused to cry. Not after all the tears she'd shed. She was done. D-O-N-E. Or maybe it was spelled differently. More like D-A-M-A-G-E-D. She didn't know anymore. Everything felt like varying degrees of numbness.

She hid in the spare bedroom at the rear of the house for over an hour, nestled upon the corner of the bed, her feet tucked beneath her as she stared blankly out the window. This was the furthest point in the house from him, and still the scrape of cardboard taunted her as he slowly dragged boxes of memories from her life.

"Cassie?" His call floated softly down the hall.

She remained quiet, unwilling to see him again. She had no more time for his pity. Or the pain he inflicted.

"Cassie? I'm done."

She sighed. He was done. They were done. Everything was done.

"Okay," she called out, unmoving. "I guess I'll see you around."

She held her breath, waiting for the front door to close. When the sound of his footsteps approached, echoing up the hall, her heart climbed to her throat. She pushed from the bed, scooting to the window to pretend she'd been caught staring at something fascinating as his frame came to stand in the doorway.

"I'm leaving now."

She nodded again. Leaving here. Leaving her. "Good luck with everything." The words burned her throat.

"Are you okay?"

His tone mocked her. Their marriage, too. Of course she wasn't okay. He shouldn't be either.

"Peachy," she drawled.

He approached, his broad shoulders taking up her peripheral vision. "Is there anything you want me to do while I'm here?"

Hold me. Love me. Stay. "I think you've done enough."

The room fell silent, the cloying thickness of memories filling the small space. She wanted to open her mouth, to remind him of all the precious moments he'd ruined with his

144

recent actions. He'd tainted it all. Nothing was left unscathed. She didn't even know if anything they shared was real.

"I never wanted it to end this way." He came to stand in front of her, cocking his hip against the windowsill. "I didn't want to hurt you."

"Really?" She turned her focus to him. "I've never been hurt more than what you've put me through in the last few weeks. Three nights ago, you used my love for you against me, tied me to a bed and left me there, humiliated and more devastated than the day you arranged for a stranger to give me the divorce papers."

"I know." His forehead creased into a mass of tension lines. "I hate myself for what I've done."

She hated him even more. And she still loved him all the same.

"Then why do it? Why tear apart everything we had?"

He glanced away, focusing out the window. He had something to say, she could see it in the strain of his features. Yet, his lips didn't move.

"I guess you can tell Leo and Brute," she seethed. "You just can't tell—"

"You deserve better," he growled.

She jerked back. "Do you think our relationship was that bad? That we couldn't have worked through whatever this problem is together?" It seemed a vivid black-and-white scenario to her—you talked through issues and resolved them, or you kept them bottled up and slowly drowned. "Did you have that little faith in us that you couldn't even discuss it with me?"

"No." His tone was sharp. "Being with you was everything to me. It always will be, Cass. I just can't risk hurting you anymore."

The tension in his features increased. He wasn't lying, she

knew that much. "Then tell me. Explain." She stepped forward, unable to resist his sorrow. "I know our marriage is over. We're done. Just please tell me why."

He reached out a hand, stroked his calloused finger along her jawline. Her skin tingled along the trail of his touch, every nerve awakening while her heart ached for more.

"I shouldn't have come today." He streaked his other hand down her cheek, killing her with kindness. "Going to sleep at night, knowing you hate me is the worst feeling in the world. I knew once I saw you again I'd succumb to my own selfish need to touch you."

Cassie closed her eyes. *This* was her husband. *This* was the man she'd married. With his heart on his sleeve and his love pulsing from him in waves, he made her toes curl with his affection. "Go on," she whispered, opening her eyes to his dark gaze.

"You're right about me holding on to my guilt. I hated myself for not protecting you in Tampa. And I loathed myself even more for not being able to help you after."

"We could've gotten through it, if only you'd talked to me."

He inclined his head. "Maybe. But you never should've been there. My stupidity could've cost you everything."

"Could've, but it didn't." The words were a breathy exhale. She needed to know what haunted him, only the agony in his eyes made her second-guess if she really wanted to know. "You're still not going to tell me, are you?"

"No."

She winced, and scooted back to sit on the windowsill to space herself from the burn. His admission broke her heart. Collapsed her chest. "I need to know what you're going through, Tate. I need to know what's dragging you away."

Her nose began to burn, her vision blurred. She still refused to cry. There was nothing tears could do to stop the damage that had already occurred. But everything inside her ached with the unfairness of what had happened.

"I do love you, Cass. But our marriage is over."

The reminder of his love hurt more now than ever. They'd done so many things wrong. From the night of the club, to the way they reacted, to the underhanded way she'd first entered Vault of Sin, and everything in between. It was a tangled mess. One that would never unravel.

"But I..." She didn't know what to say. She wrapped her arms around herself, wishing she had more will to fight. "What if—"

"No." He gave a sad smile, announcing a myriad of emotions in one simple glance. "Please don't fight this anymore. I can't take it."

She tried to mimic his calm, and was sure she came up short. It wasn't easy when her insides were putty and the pounding in her veins felt like the world was going to end. She needed to touch him. Just once. To feel the strength under her palm and the heat to warm her frigid soul. She reached for him, running her fingers over his chest, sinking under the hypnotizing beat of his heart.

"I won't stop loving you." She continued to cling to his shirt, bowing her head to his shoulder. She closed her eyes, sinking into the rhythm of his heartbeat, wishing they were in another place and another time.

"I know. But will you ever forgive me?"

His whisper spread right through her, touching every nerve. She squeezed her eyes, gripping the material in her fists until her knuckles hurt. "I don't know."

There was so much to forgive—the way he'd shut her out for months after their trip to Tampa, the way he'd tied her to the bed in Vault of Sin and left her blanketed in humiliation, and most of all, the unanswered questions.

"I'm so sorry, Cass. I wish I knew how to explain my guilt

so you would understand." His breath brushed her ear, his lips a delicate caress against her skin. "I never should've introduced you to all this. I should've been happy with what we had."

If only they hadn't pushed the boundaries. If only she hadn't enjoyed it enough to want more. If only they weren't lost to breathtaking, heart-palpitating love, none of this would've happened.

If only.

She pulled back, her fingers still tangled in his shirt. "Your lifestyle choices were what I chose for myself, too. I wanted everything you offered. I would've told you if I didn't."

He winced, the harshness crumpling his strong features into something heartbreakingly vulnerable. "I wish..." He sighed. "I should go."

He moved to pull away and she increased her grip. Yes, this was goodbye, but she couldn't lose his warmth just yet. She needed to hold him, to breathe deep of his scent so her memory never faded.

He was beautiful. His face a picture of torture and devotion. Grief and adoration. She loved this man. Always would. And now she had to let him go.

"Goodbye, Tate." She leaned into him, brushing her mouth over his. The delicate sweep scorched her all the way to the tips of her toes. It was exquisite in its softness. A purely instinctual glide of lips.

He returned her affection, sinking between her thighs, weaving a hand around her neck. She knew this was goodbye. The end. And still, she couldn't stop herself from deepening the connection, sliding her tongue into his mouth.

Her fingers gripped tighter on his shirt, her body unable to get close enough, her heart too far away. She adored this man. Always would. But they were over now. This was all they had left.

She moaned against his mouth, kissing him harder. The parts of her soul that had died when he'd walked from her life reawakened with the force of a million tiny nerve explosions. He was everywhere—in her mind, in her heart, his taste on her lips, his love in her veins.

She couldn't get enough.

He groaned and pulled back, snapping her from the pleasured daze. His eyes were filled with heat, his breath coming in short, shallow pants. He was on the brink, just like her. Wanting to take this further, yet needing to walk away.

"This is the end, Cass. I don't want to give you the wrong impression."

"I know," she spoke against his lips. "But I'm already dead inside. Make me feel alive again, one last time."

He closed his eyes, his forehead etched with lines of pain as he winced. When he looked at her again, she glimpsed determination. Desire. Passion so wild and unrestrained that it caught her off-guard when he slammed his lips back against hers.

He grabbed her hips and yanked her forward to the edge of the windowsill, his body sinking between her thighs. "God, I'll miss you."

She released his shirt, sinking her hands into the lengths of his hair like she'd done so many times before. "Make love to me, T.J."

He growled and shook his head.

"Please." She met his gaze, showing him the resignation she felt for their marriage. She knew it was over. He'd never let her jeopardize her future, even if she weighed up the risks and threw caution to the wind.

"I don't want you to think—"

"We're over, T.J." She kissed the side of his lips, his cheek, his earlobe. "Show me how much you love me before you leave."

He froze, his spine stiff as her pulse echoed in her ears. *Please don't walk away.*

"I'll love you forever." The clatter of his belt was a melodic frenzy, followed by the grate of his zipper.

She pulled at his shirt, tugged it over his head and let it fall to the floor. He was more defined than she remembered. His muscles were honed, his skin taut and inviting.

She grappled for the waistband of his boxer briefs and yanked them forward to expose the tip of the erection begging to be freed. Her mouth watered at the sight of it. The thick, bulbous head she wanted to get her mouth around.

"Cass..." He scrunched the material of her dress, tugging it up her thighs. "I haven't had sex in a long time. I haven't been with anyone but you."

She grinned, enjoying his pained lack of self-control.

"You think this is funny?" he taunted, hitching a finger under the crotch of her panties. "You seem just as defenseless, pretty lady."

She nodded, jolting her hips toward his touch, striving for the briefest glimpse of penetration to sooth the ache in her pussy. "I've never wanted you inside me as much as I do right now."

She lifted her dress over her head and threw the material aimlessly. She didn't care if the neighbors could see her in her underwear. Instead, she sank under the spell of lust and love her husband was bathing her in, refusing to believe this was the end.

"You're still the most beautiful woman I've ever seen."

Her heart fluttered. "I guess you still don't get out much."

"I get out just fine, thank you," he growled, reaching around her back to unclasp her bra.

Her breasts fell free, tingling under the admiration of his gaze. He descended upon her, taking her hardened nipple in his mouth, lavishing it with his tongue in an intricate pattern that tore a whimper from her lips.

"I need these off." He yanked her panties down as he moved to the other breast, paying it the same attention.

She lifted her ass off the windowsill, one hand on the frame, the other clutching his neck while he tugged the last item of clothing down her legs to fall to the floor.

"Spread your thighs," he demanded. "One foot up on the sill."

Her core clenched at his command. "I'm not as flexible as I used to be."

"Sure you are. You just need the temptation of an orgasm to test yourself."

There he was, the man who pushed her boundaries. The one who didn't take no for an answer when it came to pleasure. She tilted her hips and lifted one foot to let it rest on the windowsill, baring herself completely.

He stepped back, taking in the sight of her, his chest rising and falling with fevered breaths. "Jesus fucking Christ."

He sank to his knees, tearing a gasp from her throat as he roughly wove his arms around her legs and lowered his head between her thighs. He wasn't timid. He wasn't kind. He devoured her, his tongue lapping her sex and parting her pussy lips to taste her arousal.

She squeezed her eyes shut, focusing on the sweep of his mouth, the rough graze of stubble against her skin. His grip tightened, the dominant grasp of his hands on her thighs adding to the ease in which she submitted to him.

She was at his mercy. A mere leaf up against the harshest northern wind.

"T.J." She reached out a hand, searching for stability and grasping nothing but air. Her pussy was throbbing. Deep down inside her, every nerve was pulsing, poised, waiting for that next brief swipe of his tongue over her clit.

Then he stopped, leaving her panting, her lungs threatening to explode as he stood and shucked his jeans. The remains of his clothes fell to the floor at his feet. He was glorious. His chest heaving, his eyes feral. He appraised her again, taking his time while his cock pulsed against the slight patch of hair leading to his naval.

"Having second thoughts?" She cocked a brow and swallowed over the dryness in her throat.

"Actually." He cleared his throat. "I'm devoid of thought. Your beauty makes it hard to think."

She smiled and leaned forward, swinging her arm around his neck to pull him against her body. There was the briefest moment as he lowered to kiss her, mere seconds when their passion-filled gazes collided, that their connection flung her into the past.

This was perfection.

Bliss on every level, emotional and physical.

She kissed him, hard, and moaned at the taste of her pleasure on his lips. The sun beat down on her back, but it was his chest, the skin radiating with heat that warmed her from the inside out.

She needed more of him. She needed everything.

"I have to have you." Her ass was poised on the edge of the windowsill, his erection rubbing against her pussy.

He slid his hand between them, positioning his cock at her entrance. The briefest glide of his length over her sex made her whimper. The memories of what he could do to her already had her poised on the brink of orgasm.

He paused, no doubt trying to build anticipation she was already too aroused to appreciate, before he thrust into her, his shaft stretching muscles that hadn't been used in a long time.

"Jesus." His voice was guttural. "There'll never be anyone else for me. Nobody can compare—"

"Shh." She placed a finger on his mouth and savored the way he closed his eyes at her touch. With the tip of her finger, she rubbed his lower lip and sucked in a breath when he sank his teeth into her nail.

"Nobody." He blinked down at her, the rhythmic movement of his hips now demanding.

She nodded, becoming breathless as one of his large hands cradled her head, the other gripping her hip. He leaned his forehead against hers, holding her gaze as he continued to make love to her. With a rhythm perfected over time, he undulated inside her. Forward, back, forward, back, each thrust grinding harder.

Her pleasure spun out of control, building with intensity she couldn't deny. She clung to him, gripping his broad shoulder, clutching at his hair. A cry escaped her lungs as her orgasm hit—one of pleasure and despair. She was soaring, at the high of all highs, but on the other side was grief. She could already feel it seeping in—the anguish, the loneliness.

His thrusts became harsh, his guttural groan announcing his release. She would never forget the way he looked, his eyes riveted on hers, every flicker of his thoughts showing through the emotion in his features.

Goodbye, T.J.

She placed a palm against his stubbled cheek and rocked her pelvis harder, enjoying the last diluted pulse of euphoria before it was gone forever. Slowly, he stilled, his hips no longer moving, his length buried deep inside her.

She savored his scent, his beauty, and was thankful for this one last moment together. All that was left was to move forward.

"Thank you." She wasn't referring to the pleasure. Her appreciation was for how they would end this—with love instead of hate.

He nodded and slid his arms around her waist to hold her close.

She wanted to remain like this forever. To continue to fight for what they had.

If only she could. He'd never give her the option.

Unfortunately, she knew his mind was made up. There was no going back. She placed her forehead against his, rubbing the pad of her thumb over masculine skin she would never lose the need to touch.

"T.J." She cleared her throat and straightened her shoulders. "I think it's time for you to leave."

CHAPTER SIXTEEN

One week later.

Cassie was back to packing boxes. She'd found more of T.J.'s belongings in the cupboards of the spare bedroom. Then more in the home office. She hadn't thought to clean out his business files or disconnect his emails from the computer until now...when her mind was finally accepting her fate.

T.J. had already changed his email password. The software would no longer download new mail. But it didn't make the old messages disappear. There were still business emails in the inbox, a sent box full of his mail, along with messages in the deleted folder.

They needed to go. *Everything* needed to go.

With a glass of wine in hand, she delved through his past, making sure she wasn't deleting anything important before permanently removing them all one by one. She tried to pretend his name wasn't comforting. That the professional and gentlemanly way he responded to clients didn't make her heart ache. She pretended until her head was buzzing with alcohol and her stomach grumbled for food.

Business email—delete. Business email—delete. Spam—delete. Business email—delete. Sports subscription—delete. Private message... She clicked on the latter, the subject —*Private and Confidential*— piquing her interest.

Thank you for your email, Scott.

   I'm sorry it's taken hours to reply. I'll be entirely honest and say I feel responsible for the young woman's situation.

   I'd like to thank you for the files you prepared and the links you sent. I agree there is no longer a need for your services now that the man is in custody, however, before you send me the final invoice for the work completed, I'd like you to investigate whether or not I could financially compensate this woman without a trail leading back to me.

   I would be grateful for any information on this matter, and as usual, your discretion is appreciated.

   Tate Jackson

Cassie placed her wine glass on the table and stared blankly at the screen. A shiver of dread inched down her spine and she couldn't deny the jealousy pooling in her stomach. Was this the information she needed to prove there was another woman? Was the compensation for a child?

She scrolled lower, hoping to read Scott's original email below T.J.'s text. Nothing was there. *Shit.* She pressed print on the cryptic message and then searched for more mail sent to Scott's address. Nothing. If there was any other mail sent to that address, T.J. had done his best to hide it.

Her heart thumped harder, the buzz of intoxication dying under fear. She'd ended her relationship with T.J. on a bittersweet note. The only way she slept at night was knowing he still loved her. She could hold a tiny glimmer of hope that one day he would wake up and realize his mistake. Only now, his claims of guilt had a different context.

She navigated to the deleted folder, searched for Scott's name. Again, nothing. There were no more emails to or from this man.

"Damn it." She couldn't call T.J. and ask about it. They were done. Over. She had to find more information somewhere else.

Files and links.

There had to be an internet trail. Or documents on the computer somewhere. She opened an internet browser, clicked on *History* and scrolled all the way back to the date on the email.

Six months ago.

She straightened, her breaths coming hard and fast. This had something to do with T.J. moving out. She knew it did. There was no evidence yet, nothing to cement her assumption. It was the ache in her bones that told her the truth.

She clutched the wine glass, took sip after sip until the website links on screen aligned with the date in the email. There were only two, with the preview text on both linking to the same news site.

Her hand shook as she clicked the first website address. Then everything in her stomach threatened to revolt when a familiar man came on screen. Haunted blue eyes, a sharp nose and oil-slicked hair. The glass slid from her hand, the base connecting with the desk and then toppling to the floor.

She couldn't see straight. Couldn't think. There were only memories, vivid recollections, as she blinked her eyes to focus.

Serial Rapist Back Behind Bars.

She held her breath and skimmed the article, her gaze catching on caustic words like rape, brutal, hospitalized, forty-year sentence. She pushed from the chair, stumbled back and covered her mouth to fight the nausea creeping up her throat.

Nothing could stop the onslaught assailing her. Tears fell without her permission. Her chest threatened to explode. A woman had been raped. An innocent young woman had had her life ruined by the same man who'd assaulted Cassie, and it had happened only six months ago.

She stumbled from the room and ran down the hall. Her feet stumbled as she shoved past the bathroom door to lose the contents of her stomach in a violent purge.

T.J. had known. He'd known for over six months.

Six months. Since the day he left.

"Oh, God." She retched again and closed her eyes as the tears continued to fall.

The divorce made sense now. Everything made sense with torturous clarity. The devastation of their marriage was her fault. Not only that, but a woman had been raped because Cassie hadn't gone to the police.

She leaned back against the bathroom wall and let the sobs take over. Time passed in the measure of tears. She didn't know how long she sat there, wasn't sure when the sun set and darkness seeped in.

The phone had trilled its sterile call more than once. The television still mumbled from the main room, and everything inside her ached. She wasn't sure what made her more emotional—the woman whose rape could've been prevented, the years of marriage that could've been saved, or the secrets T.J. had kept from her.

"Cassie," his voice called in her mind.

She winced through the delirium and cried a little more. She didn't deny the madness. She deserved it, and so much more.

"Cassie."

This time, she frowned and slowly moved to her feet. His

voice wasn't a dream. He was here, unlocking her front door and stepping into her nightmare.

~

"*Cassie.*" T.J. shoved into the house, his heart pounding. He ran for the hall and pulled up short at the sight of her in the fading light. Her hair was a mess, her eyes bloodshot and skin pale. "What's wrong?"

She blinked up at him, her forehead creasing. "What are you doing here?"

"Jan called." He held out a hand, like he was creeping toward a frightened child. She looked fragile. Breakable. "She said she could hear you crying but you wouldn't answer the door."

Cassie blinked and shook her head. "I didn't hear it." Her voice wasn't even the same. It was lifeless. Numb.

"Cassie..." He took another step, needing to fix whatever was broken. After sleeping with her last week, he'd vowed to stay away, but as soon as Jan called, he'd been in the car, frantic as hell to get to her side. This was what he'd feared would happen, that he would walk away to protect her but not know how she coped while they lived separate lives. "Tell me what's wrong."

She frowned at him, anger creeping into her expression. "You knew." Her chest rose and fell with harsh breaths. "You knew and you didn't tell me." She stepped toward him, glaring. "You knew." She shoved at his chest. "And you kept me in the dark."

"Cassie." He retreated, bumping into the wall as he slid backward. "What did I know?"

She gave a delirious laugh. "Everything." She shoved again, and a tear fell down her pale cheek. "Why didn't you tell me?" Her voice was a plea. "I deserved to know what I'd done."

His throat closed over. "You haven't done anything, sweetheart."

Her face crumpled as she slammed her fists into his chest and sobbed. "I ruined all our lives." She sucked in a manic breath. "A woman was raped."

Everything inside him died. For a second, he stared at her. At the destruction he'd tried to avoid. At the pain he couldn't stand to inflict. He yanked her to his chest and closed his eyes to stem his own tears.

"It's okay," he whispered, holding her tightly while her body shook. "It's not your fault."

It was his. It had started years ago, when he'd began to push the boundaries. Love required spontaneity, but he'd gone too far. Their marriage had been perfect, and he'd ruined it with the continuous desire to strive for more excitement. He'd driven her to that club. He'd held her hand as they walked through the door. And he hadn't yanked her out of there when he'd discovered it was less than worthy of their attendance.

She'd been his responsibility, and in return, he was to blame for her suffering.

"Did you give money to the woman?" Her voice was barely a whisper.

"No." He'd tried hard to cover his tracks, to delete phone logs and emails, but Cassie must've found a message from the investigator. Yet another mistake he'd made. "I wanted to. But the possibility of upsetting her because she didn't know where the funds came from made me rethink the idea."

Her face contorted in pain and she sucked in a breath. "Is she okay though? I mean...is she...does she have people to support her?"

No. "Yes." Honestly, he had no clue. He couldn't bring himself to snoop. He wouldn't risk scaring her if she found out an investigator was following her. So, he'd made his final payment to Scott six months ago and tried to leave it behind him.

She pushed back from his chest, scrutinizing him. "Why don't I believe you?"

He winced. There were no words, only the confirmation in Cassie's eyes that told him she hated what he'd done.

"You should've told me." She shrugged off his touch and moved out of reach. "How could you keep this from me?"

"Because I didn't want to see you go through this."

"You withheld information of a rape, and the entire reason for our divorce, because you can't handle my tears?"

"No." He shook his head. "I mean you don't deserve this. This isn't your guilt to bear. It's mine."

"So, I wasn't responsible for telling the police of a crime this man committed?" Her words were filled with venom. "I couldn't have changed that woman's future if I'd pressed charges against her rapist well before she was raped? He could've been in jail sooner."

"You never would've been in that club if it wasn't for me." He got in her face, needing her to listen to the truth. "You wouldn't have been attacked, Cassie. There never would've been a cause for us to fall apart, and you wouldn't have even known of this man's existence. My decisions led to this. Not yours."

"You're wrong." She glared at him, her puffy eyes filled with contempt. "I want you to leave."

"I tried to save you from this, Cass."

"I'm a grown woman." Her voice rumbled off the walls. "I take responsibility for my own mistakes."

"Yes. But this mistake wasn't yours. It was *his* and mine."

"Get out." Her voice held less venom this time. "Just go, T.J." Her shoulders slumped, all the fight and fury vanishing.

"Cass, please. This isn't your fault. You aren't to blame."

"No?" She raised a brow. "Then why keep it from me?

Why end our marriage if not because you're disgusted by my actions?"

"Why?" She knew so much, yet so little. "Because I no longer deserved to kiss you when there were secrets between us. I couldn't stand to look at you knowing I withheld the truth, and I couldn't sleep in our bed when I kept thinking that woman could've easily been you. I've told you all along, my guilt made it hard to be close to you."

"Well, your guilt is misguided. And to think you see me as someone weak and incapable of making my own decisions disgusts me." She glanced away and sighed. "I don't know who you see when you look at me, T.J., but it's definitely not the woman I am."

"I know you." He knew her better than himself. She was beautiful. Kind. Nurturing. Above all, she had a heart that felt the pain of others far worse than her own.

"You don't." She shook her head and walked away. "You don't believe in my strength. You don't think I'm capable of making my own decisions. So, I guess this divorce is for the best after all. I finally agree we're better apart."

"You don't mean that." She was in shock. Getting over this news would be the hardest struggle she'd had to endure, and he couldn't stand to let her face it on her own. "Let me stay with you a while."

"No." She stopped at the end of the hall, her breathtaking silhouette making his chest ache. "All those nights I wished you were here, holding me. Now I'm thankful I'm not stuck in a toxic marriage." She strode out of view, taking his heart with her. "Make sure you lock the door on the way out."

CHAPTER SEVENTEEN

T.J. was pacing. Again. It seemed that was all he did lately. Each day, he walked miles in the same spot, trying to drive away the image of Cassie. Not only was she haunting his dreams, she was now terrorizing his every waking breath.

"You summoned us," Leo drawled, his frame coming into view from the threshold of the Shot of Sin office.

"Again." Brute shouldered his way into the room.

Shit. His heart was in his throat, his pulse a rapid beat, his palms sweating. He couldn't stop the fear that throbbed through his veins, telling him he was making the wrong choice by continuing with the divorce. The apprehension increased with every passing second that neared the day he would legally sever himself from his wife.

"What's the reason for the meeting this time?" Brute scowled. "Apart from the need to re-carpet the office due to you wearing down the pile."

T.J. planted his feet, fighting the urge to keep moving. He'd kept track of Cassie every day since she'd found the lone email he should've deleted. Jan was keeping an eye on her,

Shay too, and every spare second he had was spent doing drive-bys past his old house in an effort to feel close to her. He'd called a time or two, exchanged a few guilt-filled words, but she never wanted to talk. She was moving on, and doing a better job of it than he was.

"I think I'm making a mistake." He ran a shaky hand over his jaw. He hadn't been able to say the words aloud all week. Only the panic wouldn't stop. His chest was pounding with each tick of the clock.

"Which one?" Leo raised a superior brow and sank into the sofa opposite the office desk.

T.J. shook his head. This was a mistake. It was nerves. Indecision. Obviously, he'd have to experience some form of chaotic regret as the time dwindled to doomsday. What he was feeling was only natural... Right? "Just forget it, okay?"

He had less than forty-eight hours to get through. Relief would come once the divorce was final. Cassie would start to drift from his mind once they were legally separated. She had to.

"Spit it out," Brute grated. "I've got suppliers to call and wages to pay."

T.J. closed his eyes and rubbed the tension from his forehead. His friends were going to be pissed. They deserved to be after what he'd put them through.

"I think going ahead with the divorce is a mistake." He glanced at Brute, winced at his furious expression and then turned his focus to Leo. "She knows the truth now. There's nothing left to hide. It's only my guilt keeping me away, and I don't think that's enough anymore."

"Are you fucking serious?" Brute stared at him, deadpan.

"I don't know." It was the truth. He couldn't think straight anymore. His conscience was aware that leaving Cassie was the right option. But his heart? His soul? Every part of his chest that pounded all day long? They all told another story. They pushed him to go after her and make sure she was coping with the news.

"You're joking, right?" Leo asked. "You've already dragged her to hell and back, and now you want to do it again?"

"I don't know." That was the problem. He couldn't decide. "I don't know what to do. I'm not sure if this is cold feet, or if it's intuition telling me I need to change my mind before it's too late."

"It could be your menstrual cycle." Leo crossed his arms over his chest and sank back into the sofa. "You've been majorly moody lately."

"You're one to talk," Brute interrupted. "I seem to recall putting up with the same shit when you were having problems with Shay."

"Point taken." A grin stole across Leo's face. "So, what do you need from us?"

T.J. shrugged. "Just tell me I'm doing the right thing. Tell me I can't go back and beg her forgiveness."

"In *that* case..." Leo cringed. "I think you're right."

"*That* case?"

"If the aim is to stop her from hurting, I'd let her go. She's recovering better than you'd expected. She's going to counseling, and Shay is always over there doing girlie things. She's not dying without you."

But he was dying without her.

"You're wasting our time," Brute grated. "You don't want the truth. You want us to stroke your guilty conscience and make you feel better. You want us to placate you and come up with suggestions that will never be better than the option to cut and run."

True. All of it was true.

"But if you're looking to punish yourself, I'll give you my honest opinion." Brute's frown increased. "You're a fucking idiot for taking her to that club and leaving her alone. But most of all, you're a *fucking idiot* for letting her go. I know it, Leo knows it and so do you."

"She never asked for this lifestyle or the depravity that skirts the boundaries of what we do. And what if I hurt her again? What if I fuck up?"

"You're worried about making another mistake?" Brute scoffed. "Don't. If you fuck her over again doing some stupid, irresponsible shit, you won't have time to deal with her pain, because I'll fuck you up myself." Brute spoke without a hint of humor. Not even a glimpse.

His friend would do exactly as promised and not spare a thought.

"You fucked up once, give yourself a break," Leo added. "But if you fuck up twice, I won't save you from Shay. I promise she'll be more of a threat than Brute."

"I'll never hurt her again," he promised. He'd die before he caused her more tears.

"*No.*" Brute raised his voice. "Hurting her is inevitable. It's how relationships work. Don't even think you can go rekindle your marriage and treat her like glass. If you do go crawling back, do right by her. Treat her exactly the way she wants to be treated, not the way you think she deserves. Her fragility is your issue, asshole, not hers."

Asshole. That was as close to an endearment as T.J. would get from Brute.

"You both know I love her more than life," he murmured.

Brute smiled, all teeth, no charm. "And you know I'll gladly take her off your hands the next time you mess up."

T.J. rolled his eyes and focused on Leo. "Any more words of wisdom from you?"

"Yeah, you're running out of time."

"Don't you think I know that? Tomorrow's the last day before the divorce is finalized."

Leo winced. "Yeah, tomorrow's also the day Shay takes your wife out for a night in the city to help her move on."

Goddamn it. That kick-started his heart into next Tuesday. "Are you serious?"

Leo inclined his head. "Deadly serious. And from the look of the outfit Shay picked out for Cass, she won't be going home alone."

CHAPTER EIGHTEEN

"*Y*ou look edible."

Cassie blushed at Shay's compliment and gave a halfhearted smile in thanks. The Bodycon dress was too tight, the material barely coming to her knees, accentuating every curve...and she had many.

"It isn't too much?" She pulled at the hem in a vain attempt to hide more skin. "Don't be silly. The aim of the game is to regain your confidence and put a smile back on your face. Now get in the damn car."

This wasn't a game, it was torture. Shay had spent days consoling her through grief and guilt. Along with Jan and a newly found counselor. Sleep was still illusive, and the pain wouldn't ebb, but for tonight, Cassie wanted to paste on a smile and pretend like her life wasn't going to be irrevocably changed tomorrow.

"Come on. Come on. Come on." Shay strutted toward her car parked in Cassie's driveway, swaying her perfect ass. "I'm dying for a drink."

It was already approaching nine o'clock when they slid into the small hatchback.

"So where are we going?" Shay hadn't given specifics. A club on Crockett Street had been mentioned once or twice. A club that was currently in the opposite direction to where they were headed.

"I made an executive decision and changed our plans."

Cassie sighed, now all too familiar with Shay's chipper tone that announced she was up to something. "You know what? Don't tell me, just turn the car around and drive me home. I always seem to get myself in trouble when I'm with you."

Shay snorted, ignoring her request. "And that's my fault?"

"Ah, yeah. I was trouble-free before we met."

"Sounds kinda boring," Shay said around a chuckle.

Boring but safe. There was no more desire for fun or depravity. Without T.J., none of it really mattered. Yeah, she planned on having a fling or two in the future...maybe...if she gained the courage to go home with a stranger. But that would take time, and determination she currently didn't have. "Why don't we go to my place and have a few drinks instead?"

Shay shook her head. "I know what you're doing, and I'm not going to let you. The first step is the hardest. Once tonight is over, you'll find it easier to go out next time. And then the time after that, and so on and so forth. The longer you put it off the harder it will be."

"Fine." Cassie sighed. "So where are we going? And don't think I haven't noticed that you distracted me for long enough to take me out of walking distance from my house."

"I can't slip anything by you, can I?" Shay shot her a grin.

"So?"

"So...we're going to the Vault."

Oh, no. *Hell*, no. "Forget it. Stop the car. *Right now*. I'm not going anywhere near there."

Shay waved away her protest. "Calm down. T.J. won't find out. And besides, you can't back out now. I arranged the whole night for you. Vault of Sin doesn't usually open on Thursday nights, so I've invited a few regulars. I picked them out specifically to ensure you have a great time."

The innuendo in Shay's tone turned Cassie's cheeks to flame, the heat expanding all the way to her chest. "I don't want to sleep with anyone—"

"You don't have to."

"I don't want to cause trouble the night before the divor—"

"You're not going to. T.J. doesn't work tonight. He won't even be there."

Damn it. This woman couldn't take no for an answer. "Leo and Brute wouldn't approve either."

"Actually," Shay drew out the word, giving her a pointed look. "Leo's the one who suggested it."

"*Bullshit.*"

Shay turned her focus back to the road and nodded. "I'm not lying. He's worried about you. If you're going to get laid, he'd prefer you do it at the club, with someone who has gone through the vetting process. It's a safe environment. You won't have to contemplate taking strangers back to your house, or be enticed to go home with someone."

"I've already said I don't want to get laid," Cassie grated. This was ridiculous.

"Believe me, I've heard you. But it's a woman's prerogative to change her mind. It's just an option. If you want to sit at the bar and talk all night, we can. There won't be loud music or sleazy guys annoying us. And if you start having fun and don't want to stop, I'm sure being in the Vault will be of some comfort to you."

Cassie kept her mouth shut, not willing to admit going to a quieter, more familiar club was reassuring. It was still the Vault—a place she'd been to twice, yet it held palpable memories she wasn't sure she wanted to be reminded of.

As they turned into Shot of Sin's street, her heart pounded. "If I want to leave, are you going to try and convince me to stay?"

Shay shrugged. "That depends."

"On?"

"If you want to leave as soon as we walk in the door. You need to give it time. At least three drinks minimum."

"Three drinks?" Cassie gaped. She hadn't had more than a drink or two in a damn long time. Shay knew it, too. Three would have her dancing on the bar. "How about two?"

Shay smirked and flicked her indicator to enter the club parking lot. "Four."

Damn her. "Three it is. But I won't promise to enjoy myself."

"Doesn't bother me, honey." Shay pulled into one of the few remaining parking spots and cut the ignition. "As long as I stay out long enough to work Leo into a jealous frenzy, I'll be happy."

~

"Stop pacing." T.J. wasn't comfortable telling someone else to stop doing what he'd been doing all week, but the way Leo huffed back and forth was filling the now empty Taste of Sin restaurant with cloying apprehension. "Why the hell are you pacing, anyway?"

"Just anxious." Leo checked a text message on his phone. "That's all."

"With good reason." Brute smirked.

"Do you mind filling me in on what's going on?" They'd been seated at the bar for an hour, yet T.J. felt like his friends had spent the whole time having a secret conversation without him.

Brute reached over the bar and poured himself another beer. "It's nothing."

Leo groaned and flung back the remaining bourbon in his glass. "Can't we just go? Shay and Cassie will be out by now."

"No." T.J. was adamant. He wanted Cassie to have a few hours to herself. Besides, alcohol would calm her nerves and make it easier for him to approach her later. He'd get her brutal honesty after she'd had a few drinks, and he didn't want to risk arriving early. Timing was everything. "We'll leave soon enough."

Leo pulled his cell from his back jeans pocket. "I might give Shay a call th—"

"Fuck off." Brute snatched the device from Leo's hand. "Don't you trust your woman?"

Leo scowled. "Of course I do. I just think it would be best if we get a move on."

"I'm not keeping you here." They were making him nervous with their bullshit attitudes. Leo didn't stress often. He did moody and irrational, but he didn't do anxiety. And Brute... Well, that fucker was smiling, which was an anomaly all on its own. "If you want us to meet you in the city, go ahead. It's no big deal."

"It's fine," Leo grated. "I'll stick around."

The large dining area fell silent. Brute continued to smirk to himself as he topped up his beer. Leo's fingers kept tap, tap, tapping against the bar, while T.J. tried to think of what he was going to say to make Cassie forgive him for all the heartache.

"You know what?" Leo shoved from his stool. "I've got something to say."

Brute swiveled in his stool, still smirking as he crossed his arms over his chest and looked at Leo. T.J. followed, leaving his scotch on the counter to turn and face the man who appeared ready to make a Hulk transformation.

"Before we find Cassie and Shay," Leo started. "I want you to know something."

"Is this the *something* that's had you jittering and snarling all night?"

Leo let out a bitter laugh. "*No.* We'll get to that next. What I want to discuss is how you got in this fucked situation in the first place."

T.J. raised his chin, trying to steel himself against the punch to his pride. "What of it?"

"It's about all the guilt you piled on yourself that could've been eased if only you'd spoken to us. It's about you, and your inability to let us help."

"I didn't think I needed it." Cassie was *his* wife. *His* love. *His* responsibility. He cleaned up his own messes...well, usually he did. Only this time, he'd left a trail in the form of an email.

"Yes, you did. You've just been kidding yourself for so long you started believing your own lies."

"Fuck you." T.J. slid to his feet. The last thing he needed was a guilt trip. He'd had enough guilt to last a lifetime.

"Don't get defensive. I'm just trying to tell you, you've gotta realize, no matter how much you want to, you won't always be able to protect her. Sometimes you'll need to rely on us to help. Sometimes she's going to be fine all by herself. And then there'll be other times when no matter what any of us do, she's still going to get hurt, and there's nothing you can do about it."

T.J. winced. This was what it all came down to. His issues. His guilt. "I know."

"Do you?" Leo raised a disbelieving brow. "Because you fucked up in Tampa and didn't bother telling us. How could you keep that a secret? How could you quit sleeping in your wife's bed for six months, killing yourself with guilt, and not breathe a word of it to either of us?"

"It wasn't something either Cassie or I wanted to share."

"Yeah, well, it says a lot about our friendship, doesn't it?"

Whoa.

"Hold up." T.J. raised his hands in surrender. "Cassie's everything to me. I didn't want to share information that would upset her."

"And if you had shared that information, I would've kicked your ass to next Tuesday. Brute, too. Aren't I right?" He jerked his chin in question.

"Yeah." The sadistic grin vanished from Brute's features. "Everything would've been out in the open. We would've made you pay for your mistakes and you would've moved on. None of this would've happened."

"It wouldn't have stopped the guilt." They didn't know what it was like to deal with the what-ifs.

"No, it wouldn't." Leo inclined his head in acknowledgement. "But we could've helped with that, too. It didn't have to be like this."

T.J.'s chest constricted, squeezing the air from his lungs. He couldn't look back now. He couldn't admit he'd done the wrong thing by her again. There was too much blame already. That night in Tampa had changed him. She'd been so scared. Her beautiful skin pale as a ghost when he'd slammed into that bathroom.

"It wasn't your mess." The shame at placing her in that position, the fear of it ever happening again, had been his burden to bear.

"It *fucking* was," Brute raised his voice. "That's what Leo is trying to tell you. You're like a brother to us. And you know what? You've always had Cassie, and now Leo has Shay, but I've only ever had you guys at my back. We're not meant to go through shit like this on our own. So, next time, quit being a fucking tool and ask for help."

T.J. swallowed over the dryness in his mouth. "I don't like relying on other people when it comes to Cassie."

"Why?" Leo slumped back onto his stool. "What's the big deal?"

T.J. shook his head and broke eye contact. "Cassie is everything," he murmured the painful truth. "She's perfect. I can't fault anything about her. Even the way she's handled this divorce—fighting for me, when deep down I always wanted her to, then giving up when I couldn't handle her anguish anymore. She's all I've ever wanted. And more than I'll ever deserve."

He stared at the scuff marks on his black shoes. "Doing this by myself was an attempt to make up for all my mistakes. I'd let her go and take the fall. I was happy to do it because then I'd never have to spend another night lying awake, wondering when I'd put her in another position where she'd get hurt. I deserved this mess." And he deserved a lot more. "I just can't go through with it. I love her too much."

They didn't respond. He sat there, silent, their gazes weighing heavy on his shoulders.

"See...I'm pathetic."

"That's not breaking news." Leo chuckled.

T.J. glanced at his friend from the corner of his eye and tried to laugh, but the sound came out halfhearted. He couldn't find humor in this. "What if I let her down again?"

"And what if you don't get the choice?" Leo cocked a brow. "I'd rather go in, guns blazing, full speed ahead, than not have a chance at happiness at all."

"You've sure changed your tune since hooking up with Shay."

"Yeah? Well, maybe you should do the same. You can't protect Cassie twenty-four-seven. You need to start trusting her to make the right decisions. To start believing Brute and I have your back, as well as hers. It's not rocket science. And besides, if you don't hurry up, the decision might be taken out of your hands. I'm not sure how long she'll be left alone in the Vault when she has Shay at her side, egging her on."

"The Vault?" T.J. scrutinized his friend, waiting for the punch line. "What have you done?"

Brute leaned over the bar again to place his empty glass in the sink. "We saved you the hassle of driving into the city."

"Wha—"

"Calm down, my friend. I did exactly what you would've done if you had the ability to think clearly." Leo released a long huff of breath and wiped a hand down his face. "Cass is somewhere safe, with men we know, also under the surveillance of Travis behind the bar."

"That's why you've been flustered all night?" *Fucking hell.* Cassie was in the goddamn Vault.

"Flustered isn't a word worthy of how I've felt the last two hours, knowing Shay has been in a sex club with your wife."

"Then why the hell—"

"It was better than the alternative of them going somewhere else." Brute snatched his wallet off the bar and shoved it in the back pocket of his dress pants. "It's not like I could warn every club-goer in Beaumont to keep their hands off your wife, like I can in our own club."

"You did that?" Brute's assurances did nothing to curb T.J.'s jealousy.

"Of course we did," Leo growled. "However, it doesn't mean my manipulative girlfriend won't talk anyone into testing my authority."

CHAPTER NINETEEN

"*W*as I right? Or was I right?"

Cassie rolled her eyes at Shay and chuckled. "You were right."

It helped that the three mandatory drinks had gone down in quick succession to fight her nerves, but it was also comforting to spend her last night as a married woman in a place she felt close to her husband.

She hadn't been able to stay mad at him. Once the tears faded, she'd understood why he'd kept the information to himself. She still didn't appreciate the way he coddled her, but there was forgiveness in her heart. And longing, too. Being back in his club didn't ease her tumultuous emotions.

The vibe tonight was different from the masquerade party. Most people were focused on drinking and foreplay instead of nudity and sex. No dress code was in force either, meaning most people were in evening attire instead of underwear.

It was laid-back. Sexy. With security at the back entrance and on-call for any issues that could arise. The guests Shay had invited to *play* were also happy to do their own thing, with the understanding Cassie was only available if words of consent were physically spoken.

Which would never happen. Not only because she wasn't ready, but because it would be disrespectful to T.J.

"Can I buy you ladies a drink?" The deep, unfamiliar voice drifted over Cassie's shoulder, making her tense.

"Not for me, thanks, Luke." Shay grinned. "I'm spoken for tonight."

Cassie swiveled in her stool, coming face-to-face with muscled beauty. The man was ripped, showing an expanse of gorgeously tanned skin from his shoulders all the way down to his silk boxers.

"How about you, beautiful?"

Cassie jerked back at the compliment. He was handsome as hell, half-naked and wanted to buy her a drink? No, thank you. She needed to cut her teeth on someone less perfect.

"She's with me tonight," Shay spoke for her.

The man's lips curved, exposing a glimpse of flawless white teeth. "With you? As in, the two of you together?" He raised a brow. "I have to admit, I'd love to see that."

"No." Shay rolled her eyes. "We're not together. Just friends sharing a few drinks."

"That's a shame." The man shrugged and began walking away. "Seeing the two of you all hot and heavy would've been the highlight of my year."

Cassie's eyes bugged as she turned back to the bar. "*Jesus Christ*. Is he serious?" She glanced at the bartender for confirmation, not trusting Shay for a truthful answer.

"Definitely." Travis had a smug expression on his handsome face. "We don't see a lot of girl-on-girl action down here." He grabbed her empty glass and placed it in a dishwasher rack on the sink. "It happens. Just not often, and probably not with women as lovely as the two of you."

"You're so smooth, Travis," Shay cooed.

"Yeah." Cassie had to agree. "He almost deserves a little show-and-tell for his efforts. Don't you think, Shay?"

The ease in which she slid back into the single mindset confronted her with the force of a punch to the stomach. Had she really just said that? *Christ.*

"Can I have another drink, please?" She tapped the bar and breathed out the ache in her lungs.

"Are you serious?" Shay asked, the corner of her lips twitching.

"About the drink?" Travis and Shay were both looking at her—her friend in humor, the bartender with a scowl.

"We don't joke in the Vault, Cass." Travis's tone was low. Her heart climbed into her throat. *Wait.* Was *he* joking? "Read the rules and regulations. We don't condone misrepresentation."

"Oh, fuck off, Travis." Shay swiveled on her stool to face Cassie. "It's all about keeping lines of communication open. If you're teasing, it gives false hope and mixed signals, which can be dangerous in a place like this. But ignore him, he's being overly dramatic."

Okay. He definitely wasn't joking, which kind of pissed her off. She had enough to deal with without her lame attempt at humor being taken out of hand.

"Then maybe I wasn't misrepresenting." She cocked a brow at Travis and swiveled her stool toward Shay. "I wouldn't want to be seen breaking the rules in my husband's club."

"Now I know that's the liquor talking." Shay snorted.

"Doesn't have to be." Cassie straightened her shoulders. She wasn't sure where the confidence was coming from...oh, wait, yes she did. Those three mandatory drinks her scheming friend made her have were kicking in nicely. "I'm single, remember?"

"But Shay isn't," Travis drawled.

"Mind your own damn business. I'm sure Leo would be

satisfied with a blow-by-blow recount." Shay leaned forward, resting her palms on Cassie's thighs. "What do you think?"

Cassie's throat dried in an instant. Where was the liquid courage now? The corner of Shay's mouth quirked as she leaned in, brushing their cheeks together before resting her lips near Cassie's ear.

"I started flirting back because I thought you were joking," Shay whispered. "Now I'm kinda nervous because you might be serious."

Cassie closed her eyes, keeping up the façade as she nuzzled the side of her face into Shay's hair. "I *was* totally joking."

Was... Now she wasn't so sure. Shay's attention was nice. Soothing. The brush of another body against hers sparked a warmth inside her chest that she hadn't expected. When she opened her eyes, more than one gaze was upon them, the interest from club patrons making the lonely parts of Cassie feel adored again. "I thought uptight Travis and your friend Luke deserved a show."

"Hmm." Shay continued to brush her lips down Cassie's neck, each touch sparking a frenzy of heat in her veins. "So how far did you want to take this?"

"Mmm." Cassie arched her neck, half of her playing along with the pretense, the other half falling under the spell of arousal. "I hadn't thought that far."

Shay was so soft and unfamiliar. She was unlike anything Cassie had ever felt before. Her dating life had only ever consisted of men. And not many at that. But they had all been highly masculine partners, with rough skin and calloused hands. The attention from Shay was entirely different. Exquisite in its delicacy. Instead of dominant and demanding, it was tender and fragile.

The hands on her thighs were still, the fingertips rubbing

in intricate patterns over her sensitive skin. She ran her fingers through Shay's hair, enjoying the brief slide out of loneliness. But it was the infrequent, slight hitches in the other woman's breathing that made Cassie's nipples harden to tight peaks.

They were both aroused, no matter what act they were trying to play.

"I've never kissed a woman before." The words whispered from her lips. Maybe it was a mistake. Maybe it wasn't. Honestly, she didn't care anymore. "I wonder what it would be like to kiss you."

Shay pulled back, a mischievous grin tilting her mouth. "I was thinking the same thing."

Travis cleared his throat from the other side of the bar. "Ladies."

Cassie grinned, ignoring the warning in Travis's tone. "What about Leo? Will he—"

"*Ladies*," Travis growled. "You've got company."

Cassie pulled back, her hand still in Shay's hair as she met T.J.'s gaze from the other side of the main room. *Oh, God.* The nausea was instantaneous, pulsing up her throat as she slid off the stool.

"I'm sorry." She mouthed the words to him because she couldn't find her voice. His expression was unreadable, far less undecipherable than the impressed smirk from Leo and Brute at his sides.

"I've gotta go." She turned to Shay, being punished all over again from the understanding in her friend's features. "I'll speak to you later." On a cell she didn't have because it was sitting in a Vault locker.

She didn't know how she was going to pay a cab driver without her purse either. But she'd find a way. What she couldn't see herself through was a discussion with T.J. about why she'd come here tonight when they both knew it would hurt him. She couldn't bear for him to think this was retaliation.

With her head down, she strode for the end of the bar, then around the side to the darkened stairwell leading to the parking lot. The club had quieted, the drama she always seemed to bring with her setting in yet again.

All she could hear were footsteps—her own, soft footfalls of patrons and heavy thumping right behind her that could be her thunderous heartbeat echoing in her ears.

"Hey." A strong arm wrapped around her waist, pulling her back into a chiseled chest. "Don't run."

She squeezed her eyes shut and shrank into T.J.'s hold, ashamed and so damn sorry that she'd tainted the one place he'd wanted to remain his own. "Please forgive me. I had no intention of being with anyone tonight." Her voice was breaking. "We thought the Vault would be quieter than a dance club in the city. And—"

"We?"

There was no way she was going to blame Shay. Although coerced, Cassie had always had a choice. "Yes."

He gave a halfhearted chuckle, his warm breath brushing over her ear. "You and Shay have become close."

"I'm not going to blame her, if that's what you mean."

"No." He gripped her shoulder and turned her to face him. "That's definitely *not* what I meant. I expected to find you down here with a man, not a woman. Least of all Shay."

"I wouldn't do that to you, no matter what has happened between us." She frowned up at him, trying to understand what his words and the sad smile on his face meant. "I'd never be with another man in your club, and definitely not the night before our divorce."

He nodded, the movement slow and dreary. "I hoped as much."

Damn him. She didn't want to hear this. "I need to go."

She pushed at his chest, feeling a wave of grief as he willingly let her walk away. "Again, I'm sorry."

"Cassie, wait."

Her feet planted of their own accord as she stared at the top of the staircase, wishing she was closer to freedom.

"There's something I want to talk to you about."

There was nothing left. Tomorrow their marriage would be over. She'd agreed to all his conditions. The paperwork to hand over her share of the business was prepared and ready to be signed. She'd spent weeks coming to terms with the dissolution of what they'd once had, and she was trying her best to finally embrace independence.

"I know I've dragged you to hell and back." His voice was gravel-rich. Filled with turmoil. "But I wanted to know if you'd forgive me if I changed my mind."

She frowned at the faint light coming in through the door at the staircase. "Changed your mind?"

"About the divorce."

The light faded. Everything in her body shut down. Her heart stopped, her knees threatened to buckle, her lungs wouldn't fill with air.

"I've made many mistakes, but I can't live without you."

The words were drifting through her ears, not penetrating. She was still stuck on those four words—I changed my mind.

"I want to make this right—" his soft footsteps approached and the heat of his chest settled into her back, "—I know you probably can't forgive me. All I'm asking is that you'll try."

Her chest tightened with the lack of oxygen, her face began to heat.

"I'm not a perfect man, Cass. I no longer believe I'm even a good man. I dragged you into a lifestyle you never should've been a part of. But I still hope you'll give me another chance to make it up to you. To set things right and get our marriage on track."

He pressed his lips to the back of her head, and she squeezed her eyes shut to stop tears from forming.

"Nothing has changed." Her words dripped with defiance. "Unless your guilt has suddenly disappeared, which I doubt. So nothing between us is different. Your excuse for breaking my heart is still there."

He held her tighter. "I'm different."

"This isn't fair," she whispered. "I'm not going to live with the thought of you leaving hanging over my head."

He couldn't dictate their future based on a whim. A whim was what had gotten them here in the first place—the thoughtless decision to go to an unknown sex club had started this chain reaction.

She turned to him, meeting the darkness of his stare in the shadowed hallway. "Am I meant to take you back and forget you kept things from me? That none of this would've happened if only you'd opened up to me?"

"I wanted to spare you the pain. But you know the truth now and I can't stand the thought of you dealing with it alone." He straightened, dropping his hands from her waist. "But, no, you don't have to take me back at all. I just want you to know I made a mistake. I made many. And if given the chance, I'll make it up to you."

"How?" She wasn't sure it was possible. The pain he'd put her through was beyond words. "I love you, T.J., but I can't come back to you when you click your fingers. I can't dust my hands of everything you've done in the past twelve months and pretend it never happened. Our problems started long before those secrets drove you from our house."

Nobody could deny her commitment to him. But at some point, she had to remember the commitment she had to herself. To self-preservation. He had to give her more.

"I don't blame you." He nodded and stepped back. "And I understand what you're trying to say."

"No, you don't." She bridged the space between them in two steps. "There were times when I thought I was going to die from the torment of losing you. Not just when you served me the divorce papers. It all started the night of the assault."

She scrutinized him, hoping for once he would understand what agony really meant. "If anyone had the right to walk away, it was me. You were hurting me because you couldn't handle your own pain. You punished me—"

"I know."

"—because you couldn't..." She frowned at him. "Wait... did you just agree with me?"

"Yes." He swallowed deep. "I was punishing you because I couldn't handle what happened that night. I thought it was guilt. But it was so much more. There was fear and failure. I'd always tried to do everything right by you, and in the blink of an eye, I ruined it all. It scared the hell out of me, Cass. It still does. And I'll never forgive myself."

"If you can't forgive yourself, how am I meant to?" She pressed closer, unwilling to let him off so easily, yet unable to stay away. They both knew where this was heading. It could only ever end in her heartfelt acquiescence. He had to earn it though.

"Your heart is much bigger than mine. You'll forgive me before I forgive myself." He cupped her cheek and caressed her skin with his thumb.

"Then my next question is how can I trust you to not react the same way if I make another bad judgment call in the future?" She raised her chin, their mouths so close she could feel their breath mingling over her lips.

"I'm going to make mistakes, T.J. I *want* to make mistakes. But you need to trust that I've weighed the risks and come to the conclusion on my own. This garbage about you dragging me into a lifestyle I was never meant to be a part of is insulting. I want to be here. Otherwise, I wouldn't have come tonight." She swallowed over the dryness in her throat. "Yes, I'll be smarter in the future, but I can't live with the fear of you leaving me again. I don't care if it's for my own good. I need to know you'll talk to me."

"I promise to try."

"Not good enough." She retreated a step.

He reached out his arm and dragged her back into his chest. "I'll do everything in my power to love you more than life itself."

"I've always had your love. What I want now is your trust. Have faith that I can take responsibility for my own mistakes, and be confident I can deal with the consequences."

He pressed his lips together, fighting the emotion taking over his face. "I promise."

"Really?"

"Cassie, I'm trying my hardest. I always will. But I'm not going to lie to you. Until something happens, I can only prepare myself to act better in the future."

She quirked a brow at him and wiggled from his arms. "Well, why don't I make something happen?"

CHAPTER TWENTY

T.J. watched Cassie saunter from the darkened hall and didn't let her walk out of view. He followed after her, his pulse increasing the more adamant her steps became.

"Are you okay?" Shay straightened from her position against the back of the sofa closest to the bar and didn't flinch when Cassie continued toward her, sliding against the other woman's body before brushing their lips together.

"Fuck me drunk." Leo's words rang heavy in the room. "What the hell did you say to her?"

T.J. ignored the question, too transfixed with the sight before him. Cassie glided her hand into Shay's hair, the long strands of dark silk brushing through his wife's delicate fingers. They were mesmerizing. Captivating. The two of them making out as if they were long-lost lovers, not women who were sharing their first kiss. At least he thought it was their first.

"Have they done this before?" T.J. slumped onto the stool next to Leo and pounded the bar. "Bourbon. Straight. Now."

"Make that two," Leo muttered. "And I fucking hope not.

The way those two look together, I'm starting to think Shay might leave me for a better offer."

She wouldn't get the chance. T.J. grasped the glass Travis slid in to his hand and threw the liquid back in one gulp. Cassie had made her point. In her mind, she was testing boundaries and taking a chance. And no matter how inviting her so-called risk currently was, he'd had his fill for the night.

He needed her. To claim what he'd been missing for too damn long.

He slammed his glass down on the bar, giving his wife a warning before he strode for her. "That's enough, ladies." He moved in behind Cassie, slid an arm around her waist and flung her around to stand before him. "What was that all about?"

Her chest was rising and falling, her gorgeous lips kiss-stained. "I'm not going to return to a marriage where I'll be scared to take chances."

"That wasn't really taking a chance, my love." He prowled toward her, his dick pulsing at the way her pupils dilated.

She backtracked, bumped into the sofa and straightened as she kept distance between them, fleeing toward the back of the main room. "How was I to know she was going to kiss me back? She could've just as easily slapped me or pushed me away."

"Really?" He quirked a brow. "From what I witnessed earlier, it seemed more like you were finishing what you'd already started."

Her lips rose at the edges, and she snaked her tempting tongue out to moisten her lips. "Well, okay, maybe it wasn't much of a risk..." She beamed at him. "Baby steps, right?"

A growl formed in his chest, the warmest, richest sound he'd ever made without conscious thought. Behind him was loneliness and safety. Before him stood pain and pleasure. The sweetest mix of everything volatile and risky.

He'd obsessed over Cassie's protection and happiness—past, present and future. It was the way he measured his worth in the world. If this gorgeous woman was smiling due to his words, his touch, his love, he was a satisfied man. But he had to sever that addiction. He had to step back and let her find her own happiness. Make her secure her own safety.

"Does this mean you forgive me?" He was so close, yet so far. He could reach out a hand and touch her, to brush her smooth skin, to drag her against his body, only her smile faltered, piercing him in the chest with sorrow.

"You need to do more than growl at me to earn my forgiveness." Her grin returned, washing away the hurt and replacing it with hope.

"Make a list. Whatever you want is yours." He'd make it up to her somehow. With every day for the rest of their lives.

He continued for her, her retreating steps approaching the back wall. "How come you're running from me?"

"I have no clue." Her words were whispers. "You'd think I wouldn't be nervous after all the chasing I did to try and get you back."

"Nervous?" He stopped, unable to move another inch. "Well, why don't I start things off myself. You can come to me when you're ready?" He didn't want her apprehension. He needed excitement, love, passion and hope for their future. *Baby steps.*

She frowned, cocking her head in the cutest confused expression as he strode to the king-sized bed in the corner. He slid onto the mattress, resting his back against the headboard and crossed his feet at the ankles.

On the outside, he was relaxed. Calm. Inside was a different story. The pulse of his heart was heavy, a pounding ache in his chest. His hands were shaking, sweat slicking his palms, but his cock was the worst offender. He was hard as granite, the length of his shaft pressing against his zipper with incessant force.

Cassie sauntered forward, her steps measured and slow. Her gaze raked his body, focusing on the bulge at his crotch, then rising to his face.

He cleared his throat and wiggled his shoulders, settling into his position. "I haven't had a chance to ask you what you think of the club."

"It's more than I ever imagined." She glanced over her shoulder, taking in the room. "The bar, the rooms, the furnishings—it all fits together perfectly."

"We try and keep security to a maximum. Not only on function nights, but during the vetting process."

"I know." A smirk curved her lips and she broke their stare to focus on the bedsheet.

She was breathtaking. Her hair loose, her curves tightly caressed by the dress she wore. He wanted her legs wrapped around him, her high-heel-covered feet crossed around his back.

"Of course you do." He placed his hands behind his head, the picture of leisure. "You experienced the entry process for the masquerade party."

She nodded, still looking down at the sheet.

"Do you have any idea what the memories of that night do to me?" They were vivid. A crystal-clear recollection continuously playing in the back of his mind.

"I'd take a guess that the effect isn't nice," she murmured. "From the anger you showed toward me when I told you, I can only assume you're still horrified."

Far from it. "At first, yes. It was brutal. But when I got home and went over those moments with fresh eyes, knowing it was you instead of a stranger, it was the most erotic memory I'd ever had." He stared at her, mentally begging her to look at him. "You seducing me. Here. In front of all those people. I've been haunted by an insistent hard-on that can't be assuaged."

Her head shot up, the tops of her cheeks turning a light shade of pink as their gazes collided. "You're not mad anymore?"

Only at himself. He'd still cheated on his wife, and that was unforgivable. "Mad?" He chuckled. "Do you have any idea how many times I've had to jerk off to gain some semblance of relief?" His cock had been punishing him ever since. "I still remember your voice and the familiar way you said hi at the bar."

"I hadn't thought to school my tone." The nervousness in her features began to settle, the apprehension in her eyes softening with comfort. "Well, I had, but I was too flustered to remember. I even forgot to take off my wedding rings until Zoe asked me about them in the change rooms."

"I can't believe you had me fooled." Although, in hindsight, his eyes were the only things that had been misled. The rest of his senses had known—touch, taste, sound. Even her presence was familiar. The way he'd closed his eyes and pictured Cassie instead of the dark-haired, dark-eyed beauty. "But it was when you asked if I wanted to watch you that lust mixed with confusion. I didn't stand a chance."

She nestled on the foot of the bed, the dress slipping higher up her thigh.

"I guess I should return the favor," he murmured.

Her eyes widened, her brow furrowing in the sexiest way. "What do you mean?"

He grinned, breathing in her nervousness. Consuming it. "It's your turn to watch."

~

*C*assie swallowed and glanced over her shoulder, thankful that the few remaining people in the room weren't paying them attention.

"W-what do you mean?" She turned back to T.J., receiving her answer from the quirk in his lips.

He removed one hand from behind his head and lowered it to his waistband. "Watch," he reiterated, releasing the button on his pants and then lowering his zipper with torturing lethargy. "You scooted back onto that bed like a fucking dream."

He hitched his ass off the mattress and lowered the material to the tops of his thighs, still with one lazy hand behind his head. The hardness of his cock was clearly visible through the thin material of his boxer briefs. She could see every inch, could almost feel the remembered sensation of his shaft in her palm.

"And that finger you placed in your mouth." He groaned. "*Jesus,* that was hot."

Her heart was fluttering uncontrollably. She was reliving those moments with a new perspective. No longer feeling the desperate humiliation.

He slid his hand over his crotch and closed his eyes briefly. His arousal was seeping under her skin, making her ache for what was right before her. Making her wet for his length. She knew the pleasure he would bring her, could already feel it with the tightening of her pussy.

He stroked his cock through his underwear, holding her gaze as he did it. "I've come so many times since that night, but my hand never seems to be enough." He slipped his fingers under the elastic of his briefs and lowered the material as he gripped his bare shaft.

Saliva pooled in her mouth, the greedy need for him becoming overwhelming. Over a year had passed since she'd felt him at the back of her throat. She couldn't wait any longer. She needed a taste, a touch, anything to take her mind off the slickness in her panties and the way her core continuously convulsed, begging for penetration.

She inched forward on her hands and knees, spreading his legs with her weight as she sank between them. His cock was right there, a mere lick away. Pre-come seeped from his slit, taunting her while his fist continued to work the length, up and down, stealing a hiss from his lips.

She reached for him, wanting his grip to be hers, needing her fingers to be the ones bringing him pleasure.

"Not tonight." He lowered his hand from the headboard and delicately gripped her chin. "I want you too much, Cassie."

She nodded, sneaking her tongue out to moisten her lips. The throb in her chest became heavier, anticipation and nerves working side by side. This was her first proper experience in a sex club. The one they'd been daydreaming about for years. The masquerade party had been a job, a task to try and win her husband back. This was different. Right now was all about foreplay and arousal, heat and love.

"Come here." He held out his hand, silently asking for hers, and guided her to straddle his lap.

The material of her dress pulled uncomfortably tight around her thighs, the hem digging into her skin as she hovered over him.

"Can I hitch it up?" His words were soft, gentle, unlike the T.J. she was used to in the bedroom. "I know you're nervous. I am, too. There are a million thoughts running through my mind. About our past and our future. Where we are and the people watching. But I don't want to think about that. I just want to think about you."

He leaned forward, brushing his lips over hers. "Nobody else exists anymore. I'm done with the outside world."

She remained still, poised over his lap, staring into the truth in his eyes. "Hitch it up."

He slid the material higher, exposing the top of her thighs, coming to a stop when he exposed her black silk panties. T.J.'s brow furrowed, the briefest hint that he knew what she was thinking as he slid his hands around to her ass, digging his fingers into her skin with delicious ferocity.

"You're fucking gorgeous." He added pressure to his touch, guiding her down to nestle against the hardness of his erection. She withheld a groan at the blissful torture of his heated shaft. The only thing between them was one thin layer of material, which was currently soaked with her arousal. "And wet."

She nodded. "If we were at home right now, I'd beg you to fuck me."

"Do it anyway. What's stopping you?"

She held in a nervous laugh. "Maybe the fifteen to twenty people that would come rushing over to see the show."

His lips quirked, the unmistakable sign of arrogance she loved seeing in this man. "They know better than to stare. They'd steal a brief glimpse for now, and that's all. They know you're new down here."

"Are you trying to make me more nervous?"

He chuckled. "No. But the few people paying us attention are currently doing so because you're beautiful. You have a body built for pleasure. And it isn't hard to tell what they're thinking."

"Hmm?" She didn't want to ask. Her lips wouldn't move to voice the words. The fact they were watching at all had adrenaline pulsing through her veins.

He leaned into her, nuzzled her neck, running his lips along her skin. "They want to fuck you, Cassie." He nipped at her. "Almost as much as I do."

She moaned, arching her neck to give him better access.

Her nerves were on fire, every inch of her tingling with sensations.

"They want to tie you up. To fuck you until you scream. They'd fight to have you, if I let them."

Her nipples hardened at his words. She didn't want anyone else. Never would. Yet, the admiration of strangers made her body ignite in the most delirious sort of way.

"They want you in the swing, your body completely naked apart from the straps holding you up. They want your thighs tight around their waist. Your pussy at their mercy."

She closed her eyes and began rocking against his erection, unable to deny the friction her clit was demanding.

"They want you riding them. Just like you're riding me, teasing my cock with that sweet heat of yours."

She whimpered. *Oh, God.* She needed relief. Half her body had lost sensation, while the other half—the half that consisted of her thighs, abdomen and sex—were all pulsing, throbbing, tingling with a mass of intensity she couldn't control.

He slid his fingers between them, and she snapped her eyes open to witness him gripping the crotch of her panties, pulling them to the side.

"I'm dying to be inside you."

She was dying for him to be there, for the torment to be over and the pleasure to take hold. She hovered above him, her hands gripping his shoulders as he rubbed his cock down her opening, his fingers still holding her panties out of the way.

Fuck it. "I'll take them off." She scampered, twisting and turning, wiggling and shimmying until the panties were off. Then she was back straddling him, her ass still covered by the dress, but her sex clearly visible between them.

"You're a dream, Cassie. A fantasy." He ran a hand

through her hair and palmed her nape, dragged her to his lips. "I'm one lucky son of a bitch."

She smiled against his mouth. "Your mother wouldn't appreciate that."

"Don't go killing the buzz, my love."

She chuckled and closed her eyes, sinking down on to him, the hardness of his cock tearing a moan from her throat.

"Fuck, you're wet."

"Fuck, you're hard." He was so thick, so absolutely perfect that her pussy was already threatening to become overwhelmed. Her hips rocked of their own accord, their bodies already familiar with passion.

He gripped her ass in one hand, grinding into her, giving her clit brief glimpses of necessary friction as he glided his mouth over hers. There were no thoughts. Only pleasure. Only the building climax threatening to end this moment too soon.

Their tongues tangled, breath mingled, and through it all, he continued to hold her, his hand clutching her nape, his grip on her ass. She was drowning in his love, succumbing to the relief she wasn't sure she was ready to feel.

Her husband was back. Her soul mate had returned. This man was her everything. Her future. His laughter, weaknesses and determination. He was her happiness, and she'd make sure he knew there was never another option than them being together.

"I hope you're not still nervous about being watched," he spoke against her lips.

Her nipples tingled before she had the chance to stiffen. Yes, she was nervous, but exhilarated was more accurate. "Why?"

"Brute seems to like the show."

She shot a glance over her shoulder, meeting the stare of their business partner, who leaned against the side of the bar.

His gaze was intense, in complete contrast to the lazy way he lifted the scotch glass to his lips.

"Doesn't that make you feel uncomfortable?" At least she should be uncomfortable, right? She felt far from it. Having Brute's gaze on her was making her breath hitch, her pussy tighten.

"Should it?" He grazed his mouth over hers. "You don't want to know how many times I've watched him with women. It's become as natural as sharing a drink with him at the bar."

"Never again, okay?" She rested her forehead against his, working her hips harder. "If you're down here, I want to be with you. No more watching him without me."

He released a breathy snicker and jerked his hips in a hard thrust. "I can commit to that."

She ground into him, her movements becoming more forceful, her desire growing as his hands ran up her sides, brushing the curve of her breasts.

"I've missed these." He tweaked her nipples, earning a hard thrust in retaliation. "I've missed everything."

He bucked harder, his grip moving to her ass, pressing her down harder on his cock. She began to pant, trying to focus to curb the impending climax. She was so close...almost there.

"Tate." His name was barely audible, a mere whisper against his neck.

He growled, moving his hips in a harsh rhythm as she clung to his shoulders. She couldn't wait. She'd been too long without his love.

"Tate..." Her pussy contracted, erupting in sensation that ebbed throughout her body.

He groaned, digging his fingers into her flesh. Her name whispered from his lips, a repeated caress she'd cherish forever.

"You're never leaving me again." It was a demand. One she would ensure he adhered to.

"I promise." His lips brushed her jaw, her cheek, her lips. "Never again, Cassie."

"You need to stop the divorce. You need to make it go away."

"I will. Don't even spare it a thought."

She nodded, their mouths still pressed together as their movement slowed and silence descended around them. She wasn't sure what she expected. Applause? Cheers? None came. The club continued as if their monumental reunion hadn't existed.

She glanced over her shoulder, to Brute who was still staring at her, Leo and Shay now positioned at his sides. All three of them smiled...well, Brute's lips lifted slightly. Their expressions of satisfaction filled her lungs with renewed warmth.

"I think they're glad I'll no longer be torturing them with my mood swings," T.J. spoke into her hair.

"And you'll no longer be torturing me by living somewhere else." She nestled against his shoulder and faced the back wall. His length was still inside her, his heart beating into her chest. Losing him scared her. It always would. She could lose the sun, the moon, the breath from her lungs, but as long as T.J. was with her, she'd be happy.

"Are you okay?" he spoke into her hair.

"Perfect." She sighed and nuzzled closer to him.

The pain was easing. The mourning being replaced with hope for their future.

"Take me home, T.J." She pulled back and stared into his eyes. "I want to fall asleep in your arms."

EPILOGUE

"We really need to get these women on a leash," Brute muttered. "Every time I turn my back, it seems like they're fucking up the Vault."

T.J. grinned, unable to drag his gaze away from Cassie and Shay swaying their hips on the small dance floor they'd added to the far corner of the club. The music was low so it didn't disturb the carnal atmosphere, but in his opinion, the slow, sultry songs they'd programmed into the nearby iPhone only added fuel to the fire.

He hadn't been able to move since he'd taken a seat on the leather sofa a few feet away. Neither had Leo, who sat at the other end, his focus trained on Shay as the two women danced around each other.

"I think they're deliberately trying to drive me crazy." Leo scowled.

"Ya think?" Brute chuckled. "It's having the same effect on James."

T.J. and Leo studied the man sitting on a nearby sofa. He had a drink in his hand, and a wolfish gleam in his eye as he observed the dance floor.

"Are you sure he passed the security check?" Leo asked. "I don't like the look of him."

"Me either." T.J. turned his attention back to Cassie. "Make sure his name is taken off the list. I don't want to see him here again." Letting go of his protective nature wasn't easy. Especially not when unfamiliar men were ogling his wife. He was happy for regulars to look their fill. She was a woman made to be admired, but he didn't know this man.

"You can't deny entry to every guy that wants to fuck your wife." Brute stood behind them, looming over the back of the sofa. "If that were the case, I wouldn't be allowed down here either."

"Funny," T.J. grated.

"Not joking." Brute clapped him on the shoulder. "What's with the phone anyway?" He leaned forward and snatched the device from T.J.'s hand.

"Just having a little fun." He'd convinced his wife to wear the sex toy he'd given her years ago. One half of the C-shaped instrument was burrowed inside her pussy, while the other was wrapped around to nestle against her clit. "It's an app for the sex toy Cass is wearing."

He chanced a quick glance over his shoulder at Brute who was focused on the phone. "Every once in a while, I press one of those buttons and it triggers vibrations."

"You've been doing that all night?" Brute asked.

"Mostly." It was thrilling to know he was pleasuring her without anyone else's knowledge. Her pussy was probably dripping, the evidence of her arousal barely contained in the lace G-string he'd picked for her to wear.

"What happens if I press a lot of buttons?" Brute tapped on the screen.

"I think you can figure that out for yourself."

"And you're not worried that I'm going to make your wife come?"

T.J. grinned, still staring at his wife. "Not in the slightest." There wasn't another man who could tempt Cassie. He may not deserve her, but she was committed to him nonetheless. Her love was flowing through his veins, her happiness a constant beat in his heart.

"Go for it." T.J. reclined, spreading his arms along the back and arm of the sofa. She'd know he wasn't controlling the sex toy as soon as she glanced his way, and he had a feeling it would have a positive effect on her.

All three of them watched in silence, the rhythmic tap of Brute's finger against the screen in time with the slow beat of "Gorilla" by Bruno Mars.

"She hasn't even noticed." Leo inched forward on the seat. "Are you sure she's still wearing it?"

"She's noticed." He could tell from the heavy convulse of her throat as she swallowed, the brief, almost unnoticeable way she brushed her arms over her breasts as she raised them over her head in a sultry move. Her feet were closer together, too, allowing her to squeeze her thighs together and disguise it as dancing.

He scrutinized her, ignoring the incessant throb of his cock that hadn't seemed to ebb since he'd moved back home two weeks ago. She licked her lips, her chest rising and falling quicker, her actions becoming slower. "I think she's about to break."

Each day was getting easier. Their passion had reignited as if it had never been extinguished. All they had to do now was wait for the past to stop haunting them. Peace would come with time. But what was more important was the steady ownership of the life they led.

She turned to him, her chin high, her footsteps shaky as she strode forward on her stiletto heels.

"Should I prepare to be slapped?" Brute muttered.

T.J. shook his head. "No." That wasn't anger in her eyes.

She didn't stop her progression. She came at him, climbing onto the couch and straddling his hips.

"Enjoying your dan—"

She cut off his words with a kiss. A wild, passionate kiss that had her tongue sneaking into his mouth to tangle with his. She ran her fingers through his hair, her other hand gripping his shoulder, digging her nails deep.

"Why did you give your phone to Brute?" She moaned into his mouth, her hips gyrating, the vibrations of the sex toy pulsing into his shaft.

"I didn't think you'd mind."

"I don't." She mewled, driving him insane with the rough way she ground against him. "*Oh, God,* I don't."

Leo cursed and Brute's finger began to tap against the screen again.

"Wait. *Stop.*" Cassie glanced up at Brute, her eyes imploring. "Please. Don't turn it down."

Asshole. T.J. knew exactly what his friend was doing.

"Brute," Cassie begged. "I need it harder. *Please.* Do it harder."

"You hear that, Tate?" Brute boasted. "Your wife is begging me to give it to her harder."

"You're fucking predictable." T.J. shook his head, and ground his teeth together. "Would you hurry the fuck up, so I don't make a fool out of myself?"

Brute tapped a few more times, creating a harsh vibration in Cassie's pussy that pulsated all the way through him. He wasn't sure he was going to make it out unscathed. He was dying to have her. To sink into her.

She moaned, her arms gripping tight around his neck. "I can't breathe." She was panting, rocking her hips back and forth, snaking her tongue out to wet her dry lips. "I need more."

"Sorry," Brute grated, the sound of arousal heavy in his voice. "That's as high as it goes, sweetheart."

Shay strode forward, her slender frame coming to stand at Cassie's back. She peered down at T.J., a familiar gleam in her eyes. "Need help?"

Fuck. If Cassie didn't quit gyrating over his cock and come soon, he was going to explode. There was no question about it. He'd either have to take himself in hand or figure out a way to get his wife's underwear off in a hurry. "Yes."

Leo cursed again. This time louder.

Shay turned her focus to her boyfriend and smirked as she brushed the hair back from Cassie's neck. "It's just a kiss." She leaned down, brushing her mouth at the low of Cassie's neck.

"You've got ten seconds to get over here." Leo began counting down, his tone becoming harsher the lower the numbers fell.

"And if I don't?"

"Jesus Christ," Brute snapped. "Would you take this somewhere else? Can't you see I'm trying to work my magic here?"

Shay held up her hands in surrender and sauntered toward Leo, taking her steps nice and slow. "You're on your own, Cass."

Cassie whimpered, once, twice, then sunk her teeth into T.J.'s neck as every muscle in her body clung to him, holding tight. She stopped breathing. Then her body began to shudder, the orgasm hitting her as she rocked into him.

Breathe. Focus. Do not come. Do. Not. Come.

"Just think of me, buddy," Brute whispered in his ear.

That did the trick. Somewhat. He glanced over his shoulder and snatched his phone back, lowering the vibration settings as Cassie began to settle in to his chest, her exhalations a constant stroke over his skin.

He closed the app, locked his phone and threw it onto the seat at his side, mere inches from Leo who now had his girlfriend straddling his lap. Their mouths were joined, their bodies chest to chest as Leo cupped Shay's face in his hands.

"This is getting old." Brute huffed. "I need to go get laid before we close up. I'll see you all later."

T.J. inclined his head and clutched the woman in his arms tightly. He held her close, enjoying the adoration that took over the need for pleasure. They weren't back to normal. They were back at the beginning. Going on date nights, reigniting puppy love and mixing it with the years of commitment they already had.

It was a blessed combination.

"Let's go home," he spoke into her hair.

She pushed her hands against his chest and pulled back to stare at him. "You don't want to stay?"

"Not tonight." He shook his head. They had years to spend in here. To have fun with friends and strangers. He wanted to be greedy. For the rest of the night, he would have her all to himself. And maybe every other night until she grew tired of his affection. "I want to take you home and show you just how much I love you."

Her eyes twinkled. "You haven't stopped doing that for the last three weeks."

"No." He smiled, brushing his lips over hers. "And I never will."

ABOUT THE AUTHOR

Eden Summers is a true blue Aussie, living in regional New South Wales with her two energetic young boys and a quick witted husband.

In late 2010, Eden's romance obsession could no longer be sated by reading alone, so she decided to give voice to the sexy men and sassy women in her mind.

Eden can't resist alpha dominance, dark features and sarcasm in her fictional heroes and loves a strong heroine who knows when to bite her tongue but also serves retribution with a feminine smile on her face.

If you'd like access to exclusive information and giveaways, visit Eden Summers' website and join her newsletter.

For more information:
www.edensummers.com
eden@edensummers.com